TO END A
BLOODLINE

Revenge wasn't a strong
enough emotion for Luna –
her hatred was entrenched
in her soul, if she had one.
She would make him pay.
His entire family would pay
for his sins. If it takes her
entire life, she will wipe away
any existence of his.

By Thomas R. Hendrick

To End a Bloodline

By Thomas R. Hendrick

To my wife Lin,

Husband and wife we will always be ~

But if, by chance, we disagree, I'll still love you and you'll love me.

Thanks for growing old with me.

Thanks to Erin M., Kendra H., Alyssa B., Robin R., Charles Y., Elizabeth M., Steve S., and Bear M., for the support along the way and Uncle No No for the artwork.

Chapter 1

Current Day ~ <u>Early 1980's</u>

The tan colored walls were splattered with blood and her head was hanging off the edge of the bed. Her neck was sliced and the blood had dripped down her hair and pooled in the white carpet. Of all the years he had looked at crime scenes, this was one of the most ghastly. Detective Ackerman's eyes were fixed upon the lifeless actress. He knew who she was. Everyone in the room knew.

Sam Ackerman was no rookie, having just over 18 years with the department. He'd spent the last 13 years with Homicide. Sam was one of the best. Rugged good looks that his buddies in the department gave him a hard time about, telling him he looked like Warren Beatty in his younger days or at least close cousins. His body was worn out but his experience was invaluable. Before working for the department he was highly decorated in the U.S. Army, infantry, 1st Calvary Division out of Fort Hood, Texas. It just made sense that he became a cop when he stepped out of a uniform and into civilian life. Even with all of his training in deductive reasoning, he's probably forgotten more of it than what his collective team knows. Albeit cliché, it still rings true. Everyone is born with five senses; however, Sam had honed his ability to deduce into a sixth sense and had solved almost all of his cases. In today's world of crime and the mass amount of criminals in this place, who can say that? Several of his buddies tried to call him Sam Spade but quickly discovered that wasn't a good idea. The few people he could not help, the cases that escaped him, the cases where he failed were what kept him up at night. For those nights he used Crown and Coke, but mostly the soft drink part of the equation as he wasn't a big drinker. He hoped this case wouldn't be added to the short list. Sam didn't keep score of all that he had done in his career; he counted the times he couldn't get it done. It's the failures that bothered him. This was how he measured himself, though he never mentioned this to anyone. He was quite a bit more humble than most of his counterparts and didn't carry a chip on his shoulder. He was usually a quiet man and kept to himself. He was married to his work since a relationship never quite developed. Thinking back, the constant work that enveloped him was probably the reason a relationship didn't work in the first place. It wasn't for lack of trying; he really did want to settle down, but it was never the right time. His cases always took over his life. He was up early and went to bed late if he went to bed at all. At just over 5'10", his salt and pepper hair, high and tight, was covered by an old-style fedora, just like his dad's, and he rarely left home without it. His dad's fedora sat at home on the mantel as a daily reminder of his hero. He prayed a lot and focused on his work.

"The cut appears to be drawn from left to right across the center of her neck," she said. The crime scene investigator, Michelle, has worked with Sam for about a year. She was first in her class at the Academy, being the type who stayed up all night studying so she could be the best. Her childhood gave her plenty of reasons to care about her job. Those reasons gave her some uniquely keen senses, and despite her age, she could read a room better than anyone Sam had ever worked with. She could mentally see the crime playing out in her head based on the evidence in the room. Her mind would picture the characters' movements as if she were dreaming. She has an intense ability for deductive reasoning. She is very logical and one would think she was related to Spock, yet she is able to communicate without sounding like a Vulcan. She is a very petite Asian. Her appearance wasn't striking. She was simple and plain – she could disappear in a crowded room which is exactly what Sam liked about her. She is also an expert marksman, though rarely has to show her skills in her current position with the department.

"Okay, Boss. They scuffled in several places in this room, but this is where she took her last stand. Literally. The killer most likely did not stand behind her. It appears as if they were fighting face-to-face there on the far side of the bed." Michelle was pointing directly where she was talking about. "She was probably pushed backward after her throat was slit. Blood splatter patterns over her right shoulder show the direction trail. I would surmise that the perpetrator was right-handed. He or she, but more than likely a strong male, was slightly shorter than the victim." Michelle continued to use her body motions as a visual power point of the movements she could replay in her mind so Sam could understand exactly what she meant. She was brilliant that way.

"Why is that?" asked Sam.

"The angle of the incision is actually higher on the right side of the neck. Additionally, the cut doesn't come around the right side of her neck as far as it would if she was cut from behind. With an attack from behind, it would tend to be straighter and curve around the right edge a bit more and be deeper. The killer would be trying to 'get the job done' as it were." Michelle raised her hands and showed the universal term of quotation marks with her hands.

"But from the front, with a shorter person, it's raised on the right and it's shallow enough to show that this is where the instrument exited the neck. Again, blood spatter patterns on the wall over there also point to the same thing. See how the massive squirting blood trail travels up the wall? There isn't much blood coming down the neck and to the front of her clothes where she was probably standing at the time of the attack. This also suggests two things. Not only was the victim starting to lean back, but she was looking right at her killer."

"What else?" Sam knew she would have more details.

"I'll have more once I get her back to my office," she said as a matter of fact.

"Hey, Detective."

"Yes, Simpson?"

"All of her jewelry is still on the vanity, and there is cash in her purse. I don't believe this was a botched robbery." Simpson was the rookie of the bunch who was assigned to Sam without even asking him. He was young, inexperienced, and way too eager to chase the tires of the next car passing by but his intentions were in the right place.

"Simpson." Sam was about to lecture the kid. "How long have you known the victim?"

"Never met her, sir."

"Then how do you know 'all' of her jewelry is here?"

"Well, it's, it's....."

Sam interrupts. "Simpson. Don't make assumptions. While I understand what you meant, you have to be committed to discovering the right answer. Her family, if she has any, is counting on us to find the killer. Our city will want the killer found and put away as well." Sam wasn't about to embarrass the kid, but certainly didn't mind giving him a lesson. He was at least trainable and had good potential. Sam only hoped he was patient enough to teach him.

Simpson lowered his eyes slightly but kept working, knowing his comment wasn't exactly factual and understanding that his boss didn't have an issue correcting him. "Yes, sir. Sorry, sir. Won't happen again. I'll just say that I don't think this is a robbery gone bad."

"I agree." Sam replied slowly with a slight smirk and a head nod.

Michelle got Sam's attention by pointing to the ceiling. Sam winked back at Michelle for noticing what Sam had already seen minutes earlier.

"Hey, kid. Look up."

Simpson's eyes went to the ceiling. "Holy crap! Would ya look at that? The bloody knife is stuck in the ceiling!" Simpson wanted to say that in a British accent but knew Sam wouldn't appreciate it.

"Bag it and check it for prints. And don't forget the chain of custody."

"Yes, sir." As he looked at the coagulated and sticky blood on the knife, Simpson donned his plastic gloves and a paper bag. He labeled the bag with the location, time, date and case number as assigned by the dispatcher, snapped several pictures of it and then took possession of the knife, careful not to smudge any possible fingerprints left on it. Michelle, trained in forensics, watched his every move. He did just fine for a rookie.

"I'll run the blood type in case there's more than just hers." Michelle added as she looked around the room.

Sam nodded and continued to search the room for any clues. Any information he could find could be the key that helps to solve this tragedy. Sam did the standard cursory visual search in a grid formation in his mind. He noticed how much dust was on the window blinds, if the carpet was recently vacuumed and if there were stains – other than the pooled blood. He paused and thought there was more blood on the floor beneath her head than there should be. Exsanguination is an ugly thing. It's not always a mess. He's known people to bleed out internally. Horrible bruising and pooling of blood inside the skin at the lowest points of the body. Gravity at work. Not a mess but still ugly. But this? This was truly brutal. It looked as if someone took red paint from a large brush and tried to make a splatter painting.

In the remainder of the apartment, he made mental notes of the traffic patterns - checked the fridge for the amount of fresh food versus leftovers or Styrofoam boxes from take-out food. There wasn't much of either but the pantry was fairly full. He checked the style of clothes in the closet, noticing she had good taste. But then again, she could afford good taste. She could also afford a full-time maid but Sam learned from the initial officers on the scene that she only paid for a part-time housekeeper to do her laundry and run a few errands. Why? He would find that out later. He sensed she was the type of person to set priorities. She didn't have a bunch of medications sitting in the bathroom, but he did find an inhaler. She appeared to have been a healthy person other than possible asthma. The inhaler date was over six months old, so she apparently didn't need it frequently. Sam noticed a cameo necklace lying on the kitchen counter and it reminded him of one of his favorite teachers from his youth. He wondered if this could have been a keepsake from a family member or something she simply wanted. Sam worked his way out of the apartment and was finally satisfied he had noted all he needed. The rest of the team and forensic techs finished searching the actress' room, but nothing more turned up other than the bloody knife and a dead body. Sam made his way out of the apartment. He could still smell her lingering perfume. Like a song that plays in your head all day, over and over, her smell stayed with him.

Chapter 2

In a low-rent district, Sam was sitting in an unmarked car. He parked the car with the street light slightly behind the rear seat so the light wouldn't glare on the windshield. This car reeked of smoke. A bad habit from the guy who used it yesterday. It was a loaner from the police garage. His was, frustratingly, still in the shop getting new brakes. Sam didn't smoke and he really didn't care for the smell of it. When he couldn't stand the stench any longer, he got out of the car and stepped into a darkened doorway of the closest apartment building, pulled up the collar of his black leather coat and waited.

Sam was studying the old brownstone complex at the end of the three-way street. The iron gated front door was broken, like most of the rest of the neighborhood gates, with some of the bricks pock marked by bullet holes and paint coming off the window sills. No one appeared to be moving around the street. Even the neighborhood indigents were all but settled in for the night. Still, it was early on this cool breezy night. It was about 10:15. His eyes were moving about every three to five seconds to apartment 301. He knew it faced the street. This was familiar territory for Sam. Two years ago he caught a domestic case in apartment 302 across the hall. A very nasty case. If memory served, there was a knife fight between two "best friends" over a girl. Go figure. Alcohol. Knives. Jealousy. Not a good cocktail on a Friday night. He had learned that people in this neighborhood didn't talk to cops. About 10:45 a light came on.

Sam started walking past the smelly Chevy Caprice. He kept his wits about him as he quietly walked toward the building. He could hear his own footsteps echo in the quiet of the night. Sam used the stairs to the third floor - his Sig Sauer .357 ready in his right hand. This was a murder investigation and he would be ready. He gently knocked on the flakey, green-painted door numbered 301. Several minutes passed and he knocked again.

"Who out there?" said a female voice behind the door.

"Detective Ackerman. Is Ms. Mahalia Stevens home, please?"

Not recognizing the voice behind the door, it opened a crack, the chain on the door still latched. She could see his badge hanging around his neck. He purposefully wore it there at night to keep his hands free.

"What you want?"

"I understand Ms. Stevens worked for Cindy Southerland. Is that you?" She nodded yes. "May I come in, please?"

With a nod she closed the door, pulled off the door chain and slowly opened the squeaky door. Her eyes were bloodshot. She'd been crying most of the day and trying to look for a new job. She expected someone to show up, but not at this hour. Besides, she already gave her statement.

He holstered his "Sig" as he followed her into the living room. She picked up the stuffed animals off the floor and kicked a few toys to the side.

"Have a seat. You want some tea?" She offered tea to everyone who crossed her door.

"Yes, ma'am. Thank you, Ms. Stevens."

"Everybody just calls me Ms. Mahalia."

She walked over to the cupboard, took hold of the old tarnished knob and opened the door. Eyeing the detective, her hand slowly reached right by her own Smith and Wesson .357 revolver and grabbed the tea bags. She had already started the hot water before he knocked as hot tea is how she ended the day. She gave up drinking eight years ago. Living in this neighborhood was tough. It was worse when alcohol ruled your life. A lot of hard life lessons. Since she knew most of the people in the neighborhood, she stayed sober for her own accountability. They would certainly let her know when she messed up, and she didn't want that type of attention. However, tonight, she really wanted a drink, but breaking sobriety and waking up in the drunk tank at the county jail wasn't in her plans.

"Ms. Mahalia, I know you found Ms. Southerland's body and another officer talked to you earlier today." Mahalia nodded her head. "I'd like to review some of that and ask just a few more questions, if you don't mind." He didn't wait for an answer. "How long did you work for Ms. Southerland?"

"'Bout six years, I guess."

"Tell me about this morning again, please." He already read the initial report and did a bit of research before coming over.

"Like I said earlier, I gets to Ms. Cynthia's place every other day 'bout 6 in the mornin'. "

"Did you see Ms. Southerland when you got there?"

"Yeah. She be sleepin. I always get her laundry in the morning. I do that first thing now, cuz that's the way she like it. She gots anutha door thru the bathroom so I come through that way cuz it's a bit quieter. I always check to be sure she made it home. See, she liked to stay out late at nights every now and then. Sometimes she brought home a stray, if you know what I mean. And I ain't judgin her now. She always been kind to me." She said raising her hands in a nonjudgmental fashion.

"Yes, ma'am. Did she have any 'strays' this morning?"

"Not that I seen. But there was a man's shirt in the laundry. A white one. Button up the front kind. A lot better than most other men's clothes I wash for her. I finds all kinds of things in the laundry. Sometimes I find change in her pockets or notes and things like that."

"Excuse me, Ms. Mahalia, was there any blood on the shirt before you washed it?"

"Nah. Didn't see none. I'd hafta soak it in bleach if there's blood on it and I didn't see none. And you gotta start the soaking quick or it just seems to harder to get out."

"Yes ma'am. Where is the shirt now?"

"Her place I guess. I left it on the hanger by the laundry after I pressed it." She waved her hand in the air as if Sam should have known this since it was a normal thing. She paused and sort of looked sadly down at the floor. She was obviously getting a bit more upset. "You don't know who done it yet?"

"Not yet, but we will. Why did you leave and come back?"

Ms. Mahalia looked right at him without hesitation and said, "She didn't have any groceries. I usually get a bite to eat after I start the laundry but her cupboards were pretty thin so I left to the market. I get her usual stuff and something for me. She puts a one hundred dollar bill in the drawer just for that. So I just buy what she needs and put the receipt and change back in the drawer. We been doing that for a while now." Tears were starting to come down again. "But when I came back, she was all like that." Ms. Mahalia's face was showing the fear of what she saw. Her hand went directly over her mouth and she shook her head back and forth. "Oh...Jesus!" were the whispered words that came naturally to her.

The whistle blew on the tea pot and startled her. "Sorry Mr. Detective. Lord knows my nerves is all messed up right now."

"I understand." He replied in his usual calming voice.

She picked up the tea pot off the burner and turned her head toward him as if to ask a question but he wasn't looking at her.

"Three sugars, please," he said before she asked. "I have a southern sweet tooth." Sam stood and looked at pictures on the wall. She was still a suspect at this point. She was the last person to see Cynthia alive. And she was wondering how he knew what she was about to ask.

Sam had a habit of making himself at home wherever he went. And it makes good sense to know as much as you can about suspects in an investigation. Sometimes that made people nervous. Sometimes that was the point.

"Is this your baby girl?"

"Yeah. She's 13 weeks."

"She's very beautiful," he said sincerely. His tone slightly changed when he asked, "Where's her father?"

"Thank you and he in prison where he belongs." She said in a factual tone. "Robbed a house. I can't believe I was sweet on him. But I got my girl." She sounded as if this was a victory and the best thing to happen to her from that relationship. She was probably right. She glanced over at the detective. She was sizing him up in her own way and trying to see if she could trust this man. She desperately wanted to but...just wasn't sure. She had something she wanted to say, but instead she asked, "You got a family Mr. Detective?"

"No, ma'am. It's just me. Did you notice anything missing or out of place from Ms. Southerland's, other than her bedroom that is?" He asked taking control of the questions.

She looked nervous. "Nah." She was lying and he knew it, but didn't press it just yet.

They talked for another half an hour as if they knew each other for years and were trying to catch up. Sam was certainly investigating, but he was also enjoying the conversation. He was learning nothing directly about the case, but it was all good information about his suspect and about the victim. She talked about how nice Ms. Southerland was to her. She had given her a $500 Christmas gift just last year. Ms. Mahalia's eyes teared up some more while sitting in the old Lazy-Boy.

After a while, Sam's gut said it was time to ask. "Okay, Ms. Mahalia. Tell me the truth. What do you think is missing from Ms. Southerland's condo?" She wasn't scared of Sam, but she certainly had a hearty respect for him by this time. Her cheeks flushed a bit when she replied, "Now I don't know for positive," she stared at him as an excuse of why she didn't mention this the first time. "But I didn't see her keys on the kitchen counter like I usually do."

"Keys to what exactly?"

"You know. Keys. Car key, house key, and whatever else. I don't know what they all go to, but there's 'bout five keys on that thing she carry. She just unloads on the kitchen counter when she gets home from wherever she goes. But I don't remember seeing her keys. I'm sorry I didn't say it earlier. It just seemed kinda silly I guess."

"It's not silly. Any and every detail we find can help us, Ms. Mahalia. When did you notice the keys missing from the counter?"

"When I was just about finished putting up the groceries. Like I said, I got there early. She was sleepin' and I started the laundry. That's when I noticed the shirt. Then I noticed the pantry needed some attention so I took the grocery money and did my normal thing. I went to the store. When I gets back, I put away the groceries and then finish up the laundry. I ironed that shirt and went to put it all away and that's when I saw...." Her voice trailed off.

"What else did you notice?"

Sometimes these open-ended questions gave little answers or jogged memories. Other times, it's a verbal assault for an answer. It just depends on the person being asked. "Nothing comes to mind, but I be callin' ya if something pops in my head." She nodded confidently. As she cut off that conversation, Sam felt that she knew something more.

It was late. He finished his second tea and then boldly asked if he could pray with her before he left. She had mentioned her faith several times, so he thought he would bring up the topic. Her eyes widened a bit as no one outside her family had ever asked her this before. She said yes. They prayed, and Sam had a gut feeling he would see her again. But even after the prayer, he thought he may be coming back with a warrant and not for a cup of tea.

Sam was wrestling with this visit with Ms. Mahalia as he walked back to that stinking vehicle. He was putting together the crime scene again in his mind, adding what Ms. Mahalia just said, and visually checking what did and didn't jive with the full picture. Ms. Mahalia was there early and knew Ms. Southerland was alive and sleeping in bed. Ms. Mahalia left after doing the laundry and general clean-up, but noticed some keys possibly missing before she left. Everything she said fit. But why was he so tense? The chill of the night air gave him goose bumps, so he shook off that uneasy feeling, cinched down his fedora and kept heading to the Chevy. What Sam didn't know this night was that he was being followed.

A small dark sedan with a dent in the left rear quarter panel was sitting a block behind him across the street. Dark, piercing eyes sat motionless, staring at him as he strolled to his car. He knew when the cop arrived, and he waited for him to leave. Patient. Unmoving. Calculating his next move to eliminate evidence. As soon as Sam left Ms. Mahalia's building and drove away, the car door opened. The driver walked casually up to her building. He was used to this kind of neighborhood; he didn't draw any attention to himself. He cinched up his collar around his neck and moved quietly. Unlike Sam, he didn't make a sound as he approached the building. A small .38 caliber was already in hand, finger on the trigger. He knocked on a flakey, green-painted door.

Chapter 3

The following morning at the coroner's office, Michelle was working intensely with the details of the body. A round, colored tattoo of a peace sign was just at the base of her hair line, covered by her coal-black hair which laid just over her shoulders. 5'9". Athletic build. 138 pounds. Brown eyes. Michelle wasn't sure if it was only her eyes or her infectious smile that made her famous on those Maybelline commercials. She was stunningly beautiful. And now a fresh 4½ inch cut across her neck. The thick, dried blood that had coagulated around the incision of her neck had been cleaned up, and a white sheet was draped over the rest of her tanned body while she rested on the cold steel table.

Michelle was charged with the daunting task of recording details for the case as Sam walked in.

"Whatcha got, kiddo?" he asks.

"Besides the obvious, she does have some small defensive wounds on her arms and hands and a broken finger nail. It's all been sent to the lab. The initial TOX report came back. She wouldn't have been around in this life much longer. My initial assessment shows she may have had ovarian cancer. But due to her age, I'm getting a second opinion."   She pointed to the spots shown in the x-rays Michelle had hung up on the back lit white light boxes. "It's fairly rare in women as young as she was however, completely possible. It hadn't metastasized but it appears to be malignant. I think she's had it for some time but I've no idea if she even knew it. I'll look for medical records on her."

"Ovarian cancer. The silent killer. Anything else?"

"Yes sir. I ran the fingerprints as always, but the results made me do a double take. Pun intended," as she glanced at her boss causing him to raise an eyebrow. "I kept digging, and while it took a bit of looking, there is a discrepancy in our information. I'm not even sure if I have the right information. You'd better see the initial report on your desk, Sam."

"Well, this is a first for me. I've not known you to make a mistake." Michelle grinned at his comment as he returned to his office. Sam could sense her looking at him as he walked away. She wasn't normally an open book, but for some reason she opened up to him. She told him things that she had never discussed with anyone else. From the moment she met him, Sam was the person she would trust without question. She had a lot to learn and she had heard of Sam Ackerman's history of getting things done. He had probably forgotten more than she had already learned. But Michelle had done a bit of homework when she requested to work for him. She learned Sam had a way of getting things done. Other detectives looked to him for help on occasions.

At two years old, Michelle had awakened on a mattress cuddled up with stray cats and her own feces. Left alone by her mother who just needed one more hit of meth, Michelle was hungry. This wasn't the first time she woke up hungry, and she had already figured out the difference between cat food and the human food. Her father had been absent for a long time. Thank God for nosey neighbors who pay attention and actually DO get involved. Michelle was picked up by investigating police and was taken to a safe place. Her mother, once she was eventually found, was arrested for a laundry list of crimes, including abandonment and neglect.

Michelle grew up in a girls' home. She learned to be self-disciplined and did very well in school. She developed a bit of OCD (Obsessive-Compulsive Disorder). She learned that there's a place for everything and everything has a place. She was neat and tidy pretty much all the time. She grew into a bit of a "Type A" personality for being an overachiever. For many of the girls in the girls' home, local police knew their names as they frequently got in trouble. But Michelle was actually content with her life. The adults who took care of the children were called "house parents". Michelle's house mother, Sally, was exceptionally giving and nurturing. Sally's husband and Michelle's house dad, Dermot, was also a great parent. His role in the girls' home as the father figure was pretty average, but his success as a dad was that he actually showed up as a dad. He was involved in their lives with school, mentoring, wisdom and displayed to the children how a husband should treat a wife. He prayed daily, not because he wanted to, but because he personally needed to. He relied heavily upon his faith in Christ. His actions spoke much louder than words. Sally, who was as faithful as her husband, was also quite intelligent. She had her Master's degree in Psychology and a minor in physiology, which helped her to understand each of the children under her care. Sally and Michelle understood each other very well. Despite the number of children who passed through the doors of the girls' home, Dermot, Sally and Michelle would spend many moments over the next 16 years becoming the family Michelle always wanted.

By growing up in the girls' home, Michelle developed fantastic insight in reading people, but she also excelled in the sciences in school. Her last two years of high school actually earned her college credit, so after graduation, she jumped right into college as a second semester freshman. She just missed being a sophomore by three hours. Taking summer classes, she graduated college in three years, majoring in Forensic Biology with an interdisciplinary emphasis in biochemistry. Her minor in Criminal Justice was helpful when applying to the department. Once she was hired, she was given two years to complete her licensing to be a peace officer. She accomplished that in twelve weeks. Sam took her out several times to the shooting range and helped her qualify as an expert. She decided to continue her education by completing course work in fingerprint analysis, DNA profiling, toxicology and more. Michelle was quite good and very content working at the department. She and Sam had a special bond as he reminded her so much of her dad.

Michelle grabbed her purse, shut off the lights and took off. She had medical records to find and she wasn't about to let Sam down.

Chapter 4

The Beginning ~ <u>Oslo, Norway 1964</u>

Sonja sat at home getting ready for work. Her small 534 square feet apartment was hardly warm, but still tolerable. The heat in this building wasn't ever any good, but she didn't know that when she rented it so she kept a few blankets within arm's reach of her small couch. The only window in the living room allowed the sun to shine on her tiny Heather plant, she was hoping it would bloom in the spring as she was told it would. She had to keep it inside the apartment as it was still new, and once it was ready she would transfer to the outside window sill planter. A beautiful redwood planter that was painted white. A twin bed sat in the modest bedroom next to a three-drawer dresser, and the only picture she had of her grandparents hung just above it. She had a picture of her and her mother and a little picture of her brothers set on a table in the tiny living room, but nothing to remind her of her father.

The kitchen cabinet didn't have doors, but her set of matching red plates and bowls made the dull kitchen look rather cozy with the remaining modest furniture she had found over the last few months. She stood in front of her bathroom mirror and gently applied a small amount of makeup. She didn't like to wear it often as she couldn't afford it. However, on special occasions she put it on and it made her feel pretty. Sonja had wonderful skin tone and a ballerina body which worked out well for her since she studied dance at the Kusthogskloen One Oslo (Oslo National Academy of the Arts), specifically at The Academy of Dance.

Founded in 1856 after being renovated from an old factory, the Seilduken or "Sailcloth" campus was completely transformed and is absolutely beautiful as a university campus. Her parents didn't live a lavish lifestyle, but they didn't want for much of anything. Her father owned a neighborhood restaurant in Hanover, Germany, where she grew up. Sonja was the only daughter of three children. And this family, she would unfortunately learn, was not an ideal place to be born a girl. Her father was a very tough man to deal with. Her two brothers were his pride and joy, though they grew up with regular beatings so he could train them how to be men. He ruled the restaurant with an iron fist, and his sons learned to do whatever they were told. He pretty much ignored Sonja. Over the years she tried to get his attention, but only succeeded in getting back-handed or receiving a lecture of how to be obedient. Her mother became the buffer by interacting with him in an attempt to avoid the obvious neglect of affection and the physical abuse. Sonja learned to cook as she was made to work for her father's restaurant - cooking, table waiting, or whatever she was told. She did well in school, but nothing extraordinary. She learned to use school as a refuge; she avoided going home, and spent her waking hours doing anything she could find to be of use to someone who might actually care that she was around. That was when she discovered dance.

Sonja was walking down the hallway of the school when she thought she heard music. Straining to hear, her ears made her feet move to a section of the school she had not known. The music grew louder, as did her curiosity. When she arrived at the room from where the music was coming, she slowly opened the door. A tall, thin woman, stood behind several girls of various ages, sounding out instructions to the beat of the music. She would watch the students stand on their toes and spin around, just like the one in her mother's jewelry box. She was amazed at what those girls could do.

The young, shy Sonja returned to this musical room for several days and peeped through the doorway. She simply enjoyed the moment and could visualize herself up on a stage. She slowly rocked to and fro waving her arms back and forth when her foot bumped a trash can making a bit of noise. The teacher stopped the class and slowly turned her attention toward the crack in the door - walked over and looked down as Sonja just stood there looking up at the teacher.

"Hello, miss." the teacher said. The tone of her voice wasn't harsh as it was when she was giving instruction to the other girls. It was warm and inviting, and Sonja's defenses were dropping rapidly.

"And what would your name be?" she continued.

"Sonja," answering politely and diverting her eyes to the ground.

"No. No. We never look to the ground as a ballerina unless it is within the scope of the dance. Look straight forward with determination." Her name was Mrs. Yemininski. She took Sonja by the hand and led her to the line beside her other students.

Mrs. Yemininski looked straight into Sonja's eyes and said, "Class, this is Sonja. She has been peeking thru our door for several days now." Sonja's eyes lit up from the shock of being discovered. "Today, she joins us inside the class room." The other girls put slight smiles on their faces and all of them attempted a reverence, or curtsy, in unison to welcome her. Some were graceful – some were not but she felt as if she belonged.

"Sonja, please listen carefully and watch the other girls. Do as they do. Listen to my words and follow along. Let's see what you can do, shall we?" She looked directly into Mrs. Yemininski's eyes, still smiling and attempted her own curtsy. She was young but her movements were fluid and intentional. Sonja spent several years in training.

She loved ballet. She fell in love with it when she watched her own parents dance in the park when she was a little girl. People would stop and watch and even pay small tips just to see her parents dance. It was the only time she ever saw their relationship in perfect timing. She thought of nothing but ballet. Physically, it came natural to her. Her mother once told her that her grandmother, whom she was named after, was the queen of dancing on ice back many years ago, so she just figured it was in her blood.

As soon as she found out she was accepted to the Academy of Dance at Oslo, Norway, she packed her bags, caught a cab and left without any comment from her father. She gave her mother a hug and kiss and walked out the door. A small tear formed in her mom's eye, quite sure she would never see her again.

Several years into the Academy and many performances on the stage, she saw a flyer in a local coffee house announcing tryouts for one of the top ten ballets of all time: Giselle. The ballet is about a young girl who falls in love. Giselle dies of a broken heart when she finally figures out her lover is already spoken for by another. When her lover is targeted by a group of women with special powers, Giselle's love for him ends up setting him free. Sonja's eyes got a bit bigger as she decided right then she would try out just to be a part of the production. She grabbed the flyer off the bulletin board, stuffed it in her bag, raised her eyes straight forward with a sense of purpose, and walked home with her head held high as she thought of her name being among in the cast list. Weeks later, with butterflies dancing in her stomach, she sat in the auditorium where tryouts were held. She had trained so hard for this moment. Parts were announced followed by the person who just landed that character. So many dancers were trying out. Sonja was mortified as name after name after name was called, but none was hers. When all the parts in the cast had been called, Sonja left with tears in her eyes.

Four months later, after collecting her gym bag with spare clothes and Pointe shoes (better known to the world as ballet slippers) she walked to the theatre. She had worked out to the point of exhaustion. She kept to her diet better than most people kept to religion. She worked long hard hours and developed callused feet but everything else about her was toned to perfection. Her china doll skin, tiny waist and elegant form was ready - it was her night to shine. She had fought very hard and the tears she left with during audition were tears of joy, she had landed the lead role! Her name was the very last name called out four months earlier. Preparing for this night wasn't an easy task. The Oslo Opera House was home to some of the most talented singers and dancers in the world. She was excited, nervous, and scared, but most of all she was ready. It was straight up 4 o'clock when she walked in the front door to the waterfront building. Looking up several stories of the huge glass windows and massive iron expanses she marveled at the architecture. The large rectangular multi-level art deco building held a rounded interior theatre where she would be performing in only two hours. She was told to enter through the back stage doors but, what the heck, she thought, this was her day to shine and she was feeling lucky!

On the opening day of the ballet he stood in the foyer while gazing at the opulence of the building. It was absolutely beautiful. He had been in places such as this before, but on this occasion, he had expectations this would turn out better than he had planned.

Daniel Southerland was pretty much a man's man. A corn-fed boy from south Texas, 'six feet two with eyes of blue', as the saying goes. Very physically fit and not having to worry about the "eat healthy" phase most people were into - he ate everything and anything he wanted. He was one of those guys whose metabolism was near faultless. He had played football since he was six years old and went to state in high school as a tight end, but could easily have been the quarterback. His problem was that quarterbacks rarely get to run, and he was born to run. He loved it. He graduated as the salutatorian, which was right where he wanted. Valedictorian was required to give a speech and had some other responsibilities after graduation that he simply didn't care about, but both got full-ride scholarship to college. He was awarded a football scholarship anyway, and decided to go to Texas Tech University where he majored in engineering with a minor in German. Actually, learning any language was easy for Danny, as his friends called him. It just came natural to him. At one point he thought of majoring in English Literature but as this talent came so natural to him, it wasn't a challenge. He set a few school records in football, but nothing too extravagant. He maintained his propensity to excel, but purposefully backed off so as to not be the center of attention. He didn't like that – having the attention on him. He didn't care to be the Ring Master in the center circle of a circus. Too many eyes on him, he thought. Too much attention. No, that was not was he wanted.

Right out of college, Danny knew he wanted travel the world and a career in the military would certainly accomplish this goal. Football was fun and engineering would only keep him behind a desk. There was simply too much world out there that he had to go see, and stepping into a U.S. Navy uniform as a lieutenant could send him to places he wouldn't otherwise get to enjoy. Jumping into that rank right out of college was exceptional, even for military standards. He skipped ensign and second lieutenant based on his 'off-the-charts' ASVAB (Armed Services Vocational Aptitude Battery) scores, combined with his college scores and other aptitude and leadership evaluations. He spent four years in the Navy, traveling the world, working his way up to commander, at which time the CIA snatched him up. The CIA had been watching him since he enlisted. They were impressed with how he worked his way through all the educational systems, being right near the top scores in every class, but never crossing into any situation that may draw too much attention. The CIA didn't actually know his personal opinion about too much attention, but they certainly noticed he positioned himself in the right place on purpose. They could tell these things. They have experts in behavior that have been watching him for some time. The CIA had specific needs for people with skills like Danny's.

He now spoke several foreign languages, and was learning more using his Rosetta Stone lessons. He was a fantastic cook, knew his fair share of good wines, loved the outdoors, and recently took a personal interest in the arts. Well-traveled in his new career. For his own interests, he had visited several of the best ballet houses in Europe. However on this night, his employer had purchased a reserved seat at a very specific ballet. Second row, center section, which was perfect when the lights dimmed for this performance of Giselle. When Sonja tiptoed onto the stage, his pupils dilated and his pulse increased a few beats. She was simply stunning with her China doll skin tone and brilliant blue eyes. This woman was at the top of his list of someone he had to meet! As she danced at front of the stage, he thought she caught of glimpse of him, and his pulse quickened even more. She was concentrating on her dancing, and yet he felt as if their eyes met, instantly introducing their hearts to the each other.

Roses. He knew he had to find roses quickly. The theatre erupted in applause at the end of the last act and he stood very handsomely applauding like everyone else in the room. She walked forward with the cast and took her turn last as the lead role, furiously fluttering her feet and ending with a curtsy. She stole another glance at him as he stood there applauding, and the curtains closed slowly.

Purposefully walking toward the lobby and directly toward the flowers, he reached for a dozen roses and paid the kid behind the counter. He was a professional but tonight he felt like a young school boy on his first date. He calmly stood still and waited outside the back door of the Opera House and watched as the cast and crew slowly departed out of the building into the rear parking lot. "Not that one. Not that one. Not that one either. Dang it, when is she coming out," He thought to himself. Finally, she stepped out the door and he could see she already had an arm full of flowers. But as soon as she saw him, she stopped in her tracks – those are the eyes she saw earlier! This man she just had to meet.

He stood there in a perfectly tailored Armani suit, perfect hair and exceptional build. She had been lifted off the stage all night by her counterpart during the dancing, but the sight of this man just elevated her spirits more than anyone she had ever met, yet she didn't even know his name. Some people meet, date and finally feel they are right for each other but this…this was something more. It was also sudden, surprising, and even a bit scary but Sonja knew it was right.

"Good evening, Ms. Henie. That was a stunning performance! My name is Daniel Southerland. I had hoped you would accept these roses, but I can see you quite deservedly have so many already." No sooner had the words come out of his mouth that her left arm fell straight down dropping all the other flowers to the ground. "They're lovely." She said as she stepped toward him. She had never been so taken by a man before, and nearly laughing inside, he smiled outwardly at her gesture. They both knew this was going to work.

Gene Stack, an Englishman with over 25 years in the service, called his employee the following day after the play. For Daniel, it was a little after noon.

"Top of the morning to ya, Daniel. How was last night?" he asked.

"Perfect. I'm not sure I could have planned it any better. She saw me several times during the performance, and she actually dropped all the other flowers when I was trying to hand her some introductory roses. If this weren't real life, it would be a movie." Danny said as he set down his water glass next to the phone.

"Well, Casanova, this may take a while to settle into but you don't have much time. You have to meet the family quickly and move on to phase two."

"I know. I've already thought about that. Gotta go," he said. As he hung up the phone and picked up his water glass, Sonja walked into the room. Daniel stood up and kissed Sonja on the cheek and wrapped his arms around her. "Ready for dinner? There's a lovely bistro-style restaurant just down the street," he said to her. She smiled and agreed, knowing she was famished from last night's events. As Sonja walked back into the bathroom to finish getting ready, Daniel walked over to a small black bag, checked its contents and chose the two throwing knives and the small Heckler & Koch VP9 with a threaded barrel for the sound suppression and slid it into the hidden pocket in his leather jacket under his left arm. The two extra magazines were pocketed into the other side of his jacket. He reached bag into the bag and grabbed several 'bugs'.

"Verify Lancelot, I hope these things are working." he whispered as he placed the listening devices around the room. The CIA would hear everything she might disclose back to his boss as soon as possible. He casually walked around the room and connected them to the back of the picture with her mother, one in the kitchen on the wall clock and in the lamp next to her small couch.

Daniel turned around to see Sonja walking out of the bathroom. "Stunning," he said as he walked over and kissed her on the cheek again. "Ready? Let's go spend the day getting to know each other outside of these four walls. I want to know everything!"

"There's not really much to tell." she replied a small voice.

They grabbed jackets and headed out to lunch. The conversation flowed easily, and she found that she had much more to tell than she expected. Daniel slowly pressed for information about the family, but she was a bit reluctant to talk too much about her childhood with someone she just met. Anticipating this, Daniel deflected by complimenting her ballet, quickly drawing her back into her comfort zone. Sonja wasn't without her own questions for him, and he was ready for that, explaining he was in the country on business and that he worked in the financial industry, currently working for a very large company which sent him to several locations around Europe speaking to prospective clients about the financial market. Most of his clients were restaurants and small businesses since large corporations tend to have in-house financial directors. Sonja didn't understand the ins-and-outs of that industry, but she didn't much care. He spoke and she was fascinated.

They spent the next two months together. They loved strolling the streets of Oslo in the section known as Centre City. Everything was rather close together. Within walking distance were shops, restaurants, cafés, and more. Sonja especially loved afternoons in Palace Park, sitting on a blanket under the sun on its perfectly manicured areas of grass. He would stroke her hair as she laid her head in his lap, reading a book to him. The park had a perfect view of the Royal Palace, which wasn't very far from where Daniel was staying at the Hotel Bristol. Sonja enjoyed staying with him since the hotel had so much more to offer than her small flat. She was unconcerned that his company paid 1,000 Norwegian Krones a night for a hotel room or that he bought her dinner in one the hotel's three restaurants. Daniel would drive her to the ballet house every night of her performances, always standing in the same place near the back of the auditorium with a single rose. Daniel pretended to be on a budget. While she was at the theatre practicing during the day, Daniel would spend the day working. On her few nights off from the stage, Daniel would purchase tickets to one of the other ballet houses, such as the "Christiania Teater", where she knew a few of the cast members. On those days she and Daniel would walk in the back doors and hang out with her friends. She enjoyed that he fit right in, which made the day more appealing showing off this man in her life. She grew more enamored of him every minute, and it didn't hurt that he was a big hit among her girlfriends. Keeping his eyes off her was becoming very hard for him. He had always been a pretty good judge of people, and he began to think she had no clue what her father really did. Even with the weekly calls to Stack, who was currently based out of Marseille, Spain, he knew he was falling for her, which was totally out of the rules of his true business. Sex was fine, but don't let the heart get involved! Stay focused, he kept telling himself, but it was just a matter of time.

Stack called Daniel again at the end of the month to check his progress. They talked the whole of the situation and decided to change the strategy in a couple days. Daniel didn't want to leave, but knew there was no choice. What he wanted was to delicately press Sonja for more information, but Stack needed him to have a face-to-face with her father as soon as possible.

Chapter 5

Hanover, Germany

The restaurant was the corporate office of his organization. Simply due to the location of the restaurant, they had plenty of business and were nearly always busy during the lunch and dinner times. Sonja's father, Hugo, was a small businessman. A strong jaw, dark hair and eyes, but an average looking fellow. He had a showmanship sort of personality which made many people feel comfortable sitting at his tables. Only the men in his immediate family and his hired muscle knew that he was ruthless behind closed doors.

At some point in his life he thought he loved his wife, but that was in his younger days. His mother had abandoned him when he was six years old. She walked out of their hotel and never came back for him. When he finally left the hotel room to search for her, he was literally picked up by a coal worker several blocks away I and forced into work in the same coal mines. He was a skinny kid who soon learned that if you couldn't fight, you didn't eat. He chose fighting. The man who found him was called Jürgen, and he was the only person who taught Hugo anything. Hugo hated his mother for leaving him, vowing hatred toward women from then on. He worked his way out of the mines when Jürgen died and he went to work in town at a grocery store stocking shelves. In addition to learning to fight, Jürgen taught him that women were beneath him. They were meant to cook and clean, and to be used for sex. He didn't grow up with many happy emotions, starting and finishing fights rather easily. Over time, he learned how to control his temper.

Hugo met his wife, Brigitte, while working at the grocery store when he was in his twenties. It was the first time he had seen beauty in a woman and he didn't want to throw away the relationship. He wanted to keep her. He liked the color of her eyes, and the way she looked at him was intoxicating. She smelled nice, too. She was a couple of years younger than he when they started going steady. It was a very rough time in the economy and they didn't see eye-to-eye on many things. He explained his childhood, and she excused a lot his bad behavior. While she never knew, she enabled him by falling into his plans just for being a good woman who excused his poor attitude and didn't ask too many questions. They dated for several months, and she fell in love with him. He wasn't the man of her dreams, but he provided for her. He fit into her idea of what a man should be. Times were hard and Hugo was a hard worker. It wasn't an easy relationship unless they were dancing. In those moments, it was wonderful! It was the only time in his life when he truly loved her. He could look into her eyes, smell her perfume, feel the warmth of her body, and lose himself. She was a keeper. It was also when dancing that he became the gentleman she knew he could be. When they went out on a date, other dancers would yield the floor while anyone else watching would stop and stare as they would glide around the floor. It really was perfection.

Neither of them really knew how they stayed together for so long, but twenty-seven years and three children later they were still married. Along the way, Hugo slowly and quietly built a network of contacts and muscle. He was very good at business and kept everything he did very compartmentalized. He didn't have any formal schooling, but he understood strength and violence very well, using that as his main tool to keep everything and everyone in line. There were very few people he trusted with his business dealings, and Brigitte was not one of them. She had no idea what he did other than the restaurant they started some twenty-one years prior. She thought he went to the bank and had to beg for a loan to buy the corner store where they met. The grocery store finally closed and he knew it would be the perfect place to set up a new business. In reality, he didn't have to go to the bank. He had the cash. However, any illegal monies are usually covered up by legal transactions. Hugo did go to the bank and borrow money against the restaurant and, unbeknownst to her, paid it off within the first year, showing great profit. And why not? The restaurant was busy every night once their reputation took off. Men in the area came by to see the beautiful Brigitte. She was a wonderful hostess. She paid attention to everybody who walked in and nearly always had a smile on her face. She enjoyed being the hostess so much more than working other positions. Hugo worked in the kitchen most of the time, but on occasions he greeted people. He learned how to put on a smile, talk politely, even complimenting a few of the wives as they arrived. This did not come naturally for him and there were days that this was evident. Over time, he offered valet service as parking in the neighborhood was difficult. Not only did this increase the business but the more trustworthy parking valets were recruited as muscle, drivers, spotters, or other disposable labor in his organization. Hugo was a great cook and was very fast with the kitchen knives. He had a round piece of wood hanging on the wall at the opposite end of the kitchen where food was chopped. He could use just about any large kitchen knife, aim at the piece of wood and hit it most of the time. There was plenty of evidence in the wood that he was good at throwing knives.

Everything on the first floor was all legitimate business. On the second floor, the front two thirds above the restaurant was where they lived; a four bedroom place with a great view from nearly every direction. In the back of the restaurant was a door with a staircase leading to the basement where they stored food and store supplies. However, there was a second door. A brown door that Hugo kept locked. No one but Hugo was allowed to go through the brown door. That door led upstairs to the remaining third of the second floor which held two private offices. Here is where the big money was made, secrets were kept, and the fate of young girls' lives were determined.

Chapter 6

Brigitte and their oldest son, Dominik, were loading groceries into the restaurant from the alley entrance as they did every Thursday - cases of lettuce, carrots, fish, lamb and other fresh groceries. Brigitte counted all inventory for this order, signed off, and went inside, leaving Dominik to carry it all in. As usual, the driver waited for Dominik's mother to leave and then handed him a small sealed box labeled "Second Floor". Dominik paid the driver in cash and immediately took the sealed box upstairs from the outside entrance, placed it where it goes, locked the door and returned downstairs to continue bringing in the groceries. Dominik knew nearly almost everything Hugo did, and at 25 years old, was in charge of the southern part of the business. It was just after 8 a.m., and Dominik knew his father would be upstairs soon to check on the package. This was such an occasion when Hugo would use the brown door that no one else was allowed to open.

A few minutes after Dominik had returned, a small black four-door car slowly drove down the side street. Dominik picked up another case of groceries, as did the driver, who always helped carry. in the food since he got such a generous tip. As they stepped out from behind the truck, the silent bullets quietly ripped through the air and then peppered the wall next to them. The driver fell immediately. Dominik rolled backwards on the ground behind the truck. As far as Dominik knew, Hugo did not allow guns on the grounds except in his private offices upstairs. On a small scale, if there was any incident on this property, it would appear to be the work of a street thug or small gang, not a mafia hit. Dominik grabbed the driver and quickly lifted him into the back of the truck and slammed the overhead rolling door. More bullets came down the other side of the truck and popped the rear outside tire. Dominik jumped down and threw out a few bottles of ketchup on the ground to try to cover the driver's blood. Hugo's rule is "Brigitte will never know". It was also a sign to Hugo the direction where the shots came from. Dominik ran to the front of the truck as the little black car rolled up the window. Dominik could just make out the shooter as the window closed: light-skinned female with cotton white hair staring at him through dark sunglasses. The car sped off without another sound. Dominik started the truck and began to feel a bit lightheaded. Feeling a stinging sensation, he reached under his jacket to grab the right side of his chest. Feeling something wet, he removed his hand but didn't paused at the sight of blood. He thought that was the driver's, but soon realized it was his own. He was still running on the adrenalin his body was producing and he hoped he had enough time. He expected the pain to catch up to him quickly. Dominik called his boss and told him everything.

"We were just hit right outside the back of the shop. The box is safe, Hugo. The driver is dead. I'm taking care of the body but I'm bleeding pretty badly and the outside tire of this truck is flat. I won't be able to drive anywhere fast." he said. Trying to drive a large box truck and suppress his bleeding was proving to be more a challenge than he ever thought and he had thought about the possibility of days like this ever since he learned what his father did for a living. He would never forget that day.

Dom had just turned 12 the day before his father told him to get in the car for a ride. It was a summer day with a cool breeze. He wasn't a fan of father. Hugo was a very rough man and had given his son plenty of beatings to keep him in line or for any other reason Hugo would think of. "Look out the window Dominik. What do you see?" Without waiting for an answer Hugo continued. "You see weakness because you are a strong boy. You see others doing what you tell them to because you and they both know you are stronger than they are. They know you are smarter. They know you are meaner. Other men will grow to fear you. Women will grow to do whatever you tell them. For now, the only woman who can tell you what do to is your mother. You understand?" Dominick nodded. They continued down the road and turned down an alley.

"Listen to me very carefully. You are my son and you work for me. You are always to make me proud of you. You are not permitted fail me. Dominik, you will do anything and everything you can to get home tonight. Do you understand me?" Dominik nodded again. "Now get out. Find your way home." Dominik got out of the car. The cool breeze felt a bit colder now. He wasn't scared of being alone at night and he was fairly sure he knew how to get back home despite the fact he was several miles away. Hugo left without another word while Dominik watched the tail lights turn away into the street. He was alone now. Truthfully he didn't quite understand what his father meant except he had to walk home now.

The alley was damp and filled with overflowing trash cans like most alleys. Steam rose up threw the sewer vents. The sun was still up but it wouldn't be for long.

"What an asshole," he thought as he turned around to walk right back the way they came. Just one more moment in life to make him hate his father. But he feared him more than he hated him. He began walking towards the street when a squeaky door opened up about 30 feet ahead. Several boys slowly walked out and simply looked at him. They didn't walk away. They stared at him. Dominik began to get that feeling that this alley wasn't safe. He wasn't really sure he could just walk by these guys so he decided to casually turn around and walk out the other end of the alley. That's when another door opened up about 40 feet from him. Several more kids strolled out blocking his exit. That sinking feeling in his gut just got worse. He knew he was about to fight his way out of this alley. It wouldn't be his first fight but he certainly wasn't confident against this many. "What a huge asshole!" he thought again.

Dominik was just 12 but he wasn't a scrawny kid nor was he considered a large fella either. All eight kids slowly began to close in on him. No use in trying to talk his way out. His father had set this up. Is this what he meant when he said 'they think I'm smarter and stronger and meaner'? If they already think this way, then I have the advantage! Now all I have to do is prove it to them – and myself.

Just then one of the boys rushed him and the fight was on. Punches flew and he kicked, slapped and even bit part of a kids ear off. He stood with blood dripping from his mouth. Some his and some not. He spit the boy's ear out of his mouth. Three of the boys were on the ground and they were still a concern. The earless boy had run off. "Stronger, smarter, meaner" were the words that kept flowing through his head. He stepped over to one of the trash cans and grabbed a broken wooden chair leg. He looked it over and saw it still had a bare screw sticking out at the end. He wiped his mouth with the sleeve of his shirt and heaved a few more deep breaths of air. He said nothing. He simply walked toward the remaining kids. While closing the distance, he stomped on the hands of three boy's hands lying on the ground. Everyone could hear fingers breaking. At each step, his chest heaved bigger and his eyes focused on his way out. The problem was the other kids were in the way of his way out and they all knew it.

Just passing the last broken hand, he waited. He didn't rush them. He needed rest and he wanted them to come to him. Come get your beating he thought. Of the four remaining kids, the oldest must have been about 16 and he looked like a mountain compared to everyone else. He wore his hat low over his eyes and started walking toward Dominik. As the distance between them closed, the big fella reached into his back pocket and pulled out a 3" lock blade folding knife!

"Smarter, stronger, meaner" went through his mind again and "no such thing as a fair fight". Dominik stopped, took a few steps back and grabbed another broken chair leg but this one didn't have a screw sticking out. Two of the kids rushed him and the fight continued. One was taking out quickly. Then, while he swung away with the chair legs in a very clumsy way, he managed to get one of them knocked out of his hand at the same time a fist came crushing in to his shoulder. He concentrated on the knife. But biggest threat to him at the moment was Mountain Boy's foot which was rearing back for what would be a painful kick. Instead of fighting the momentum of the last shoulder punch, he rolled in the same direction and the kid followed with him but Dominik rolled onto his feet and came up and swinging the chair leg hitting that kid square in the jaw. Mountain Boy's foot missed. Two more down and two to go. Mountain Boy's friend was a skinny kid but seemed very fast. He had tiny hands and smelled just like this alley trash as if he lived here. Was he protecting his home? Was he homeless? His steely blue eyes were fixated on Dominik when Mountain Boy decided to try another kick and Dominik's right hand came up just in time to slam the exposed screw right in the top of his knee. It connected so hard the chair leg was pulled out of Dominik's hand as he fell to the ground. The knife was free and two remaining foes both came to the same conclusion. It could be a race to see who gets it first. But it wasn't. The fight left the kid when Mountain Boy fell. He looked around and saw several tough kids were lying on the ground and the others had crawled or ran away.

Dominik began walking to the street. When Dominik was just about to turn the corner onto the sidewalk, he turned and hollered at the still standing kid. The smallest of the bunch.

"Hey kid. Take your hat off." The kid did as he was told. He stood there nearly shaking. Dominik looked at the kid. Dirty. Smelly. Probably hungry. A little sliver of white hair across his brow. Odd looking kid. "I might be back. You let them know. Understand?"

The kid nodded just as his did a little less than an hour ago to his father. "Smarter, stronger, meaner' went through his mind again. "He's still an asshole," he murmured out loud this time.

Dominik's pain level increased bringing him out of the memory and back into concentrating his driving. The bullet had passed all the way through his torso just under his right lung.

"Go to the doctor. You know the one to see at the hospital. I'll call and tell him you're on the way. Who was it?"

"Small black four-door car; blacked-out windows. No plates that I could see. The finger was a girl, boss. A girl! Lots of really white hair and dark sunglasses." Dom's breathing was more labored now and his chest was throbbing.

"White hair, huh? Okay. Go! How bad off are you?"

"Pretty bad. I'm dizzy already and I'm not a mile away yet....and ...and I wasn't smarter today, Boss."

Hugo paused before he spoke.

"Do what you can. Call your guys for protection now, get a new driver and I will check on you later." With that, the call went dead. No emotion about his oldest son being shot. This was business.

Hugo couldn't help wondering about the white-haired girl as he walked out the back door to start cleaning up the mess. He couldn't help but wonder who she was. Who did she work for? Who wanted to take over his business? She obviously had training, good training. And patience. This was slow and deliberate. There had been several attempts by other small-time gangs in the area trying to muscle in on the business, but they all failed. This was the first time someone had the guts to come to the restaurant. Were they bold or maybe just plain stupid? Either way, they had started something and brought it directly to his doorstep... sticking it right in his face.

"Oh dear. What is all this?" Brigitte asked as she walked out the back.

"Just a broken crate. I've almost got it this all cleaned up. Go back inside 'Gitta. Go on now. I will take care of the mess." Hugo opened up his hands and waved her back into the shop and he looked up and down the back street.

Rüdiger's phone rang. Hugo explained everything to his youngest son and gave him explicit instructions. Rüdiger, or 'Rudy' as his buddies called him, added guards to the roof top. They were to take a week's worth of provisions, say nothing to anyone, and be there in less than 30 minutes.

These men were skilled with military-like training. Rudy didn't know where they came from and he had never seen them before. He only knew the number to call and the code words for "Get your ass here quick." The roof was already prepared with large, weatherproof, locked iron boxes in the middle of the roof. Each of the four boxes contained a single FN Fusil Automatique Leger or FAL. Born of Belgium designers Dieudonne Saive and Ernest Vervier, this light automatic rifle receives 20 or 30 round magazines. Hugo bought only the 30-round mags. If these containers ever had to be used, they needed to be full, so he stored at least 35 magazines already loaded. He was prepared for over one thousand rounds per man just to start. Stored below the preloaded magazines were several cases of spare rounds. Hanging in the lid of the box were several pistols. Hugo chose Ceska Zbrojovka CZ75 semi-auto pistols, better known as The Phantom, also loaded with their 15-round dual rack magazines. The pistols were inserted into specialized paddle holsters where the brace bracket was shoved down the inside of the waistband holding the holster in place. It was quick and effective. Finally, in the net bag hanging to the right of the pistols was a small bag of five hand grenades. Next to that was a set of binoculars. Hugo thought of everything. While never wanting to draw any attention to the shop, he also knew a day like this may come. Over the years the roof was slowly redone. New flat roof material, taller reinforced edges so men could walk around protected, yet still see just over the edges. Small cutouts were placed in several strategic locations so his men would have the advantage to shoot and still have some protection. There was even a small area in the corner where a three-foot tall concrete privacy wall was constructed, partially hiding a makeshift outdoor toilet. There was no reason for anyone to leave the roof until the job was done and the threat was neutralized. Retractable stairs from the alley and roof access from his offices were the only way to gain access, plus he tried keeping the restaurant as separated as it could be. While still keeping with the neighborhood style, Hugo's remodel was designed to fit in with the neighborhood but was still a veritable fortress. The weakness was the restaurant.

Dom pulled the truck over near a secluded area of the Leine River and passed out from loss of blood. His body was going into shock. When his three-man protection team caught up to him, they already had a plan of action. One of them pulled the body from the back of the truck and quickly weighted down the body. He pushed the lifeless mass into the river and drove off with the truck while the other two grabbed Dom and put him in their car. The driver went as fast as he could while the other tried to stop the bleeding. Try as he did, there was not much else he could do. Before reaching the hospital, Dom was dead. Using Dom's phone, the driver called Hugo and relayed the news. Hugo paused only for a moment while his anger slowly built inside him. He gave the driver instructions and took Dom's body into the hospital where their personal doctor met them.

Twenty-two minutes later, Rudy's men were on the roof as instructed. Hugo had unlocked the iron boxes. He looked each man in the eye, and without question they knew who was in charge. Hugo turned and left. He locked the men on the roof and walked downstairs to his office where Rudy was waiting. Each man on the roof picked a box that coordinated with the direction he would be guarding. They grabbed the holstered Phantom and shoved the hard plastic paddle bracket inside their waistband. They pulled out the familiar CZ75, checked to see if it was loaded, then properly chambered a round and holstered it. Each one also grabbed their FAL and checked it as well. All four of the team wore a small insignia on his lapel. The highest ranking man, a captain, gave the orders. Two of them would patrol during the day. All four of them would patrol at night. "Sleep and eat when you're not on the wall." He said. There wasn't much conversation after that.

An hour later Brigitte got a phone call from their doctor. He explained that Dominik had been in a terrible accident where he died from his wounds just a few moments ago. Brigitte dropped to her knees and cried out. Employees were watching so Hugo quietly put up the "Closed" sign in the front of the shop and stepped beside his wife, helping her off the floor and up the stairs. The lunch rush had not yet begun. The remaining kitchen help was given the next few days off with pay and the restaurant was quiet.   Hugo left his wife to cry in her bedroom and he walked to second floor living room window and starred out while silently vowing revenge.

Chapter 7

Sonja's phone rang early in the morning. "Hello?" Sonja's was saddened by the news of her oldest brother Dominik. However, of the two brothers, he was most like her father. Girls were simply a commodity. If she only knew how right she really was. The funeral was set for the following Monday which actually worked out well for Sonja as her performances were dark on Sundays, Mondays and Tuesdays, which meant she had those days off. She dreaded going back to where her father was. She had waited very long to leave that house but it was a family duty to return for funerals. It would be very disrespectful and a horrible mistake if she did not attend. She dressed and met Danny for coffee at his hotel and relayed the story about her brother. Daniel could see that she was upset and still reluctant to go. He offered to go with her and she tried to object, but he insisted. Danny hugged her and told her to go pack a few things and he would pick her up in an hour. He told her his boss would understand. And understand he did. Stack was actually pleased. This was the 'in' he was waiting for and it had fallen dead in his lap.

"What the hell happened in Hanover?" Danny asked Stack over a private phone conversation.

"We don't know yet. We just learned about this with this morning's briefings. But this is your chance to meet him. You are going, right?"

"Yes, of course. She just told me and I insisted on taking her."

"Be prepared. We already know Hugo has closed the restaurant and we're pretty sure he has men on the roof. I'm betting he's planning on more attacks coming soon. Find out if Sonja knows about her father's enemies."

"Look Stack, I've been through this before with her. She doesn't have a clue what he does. I'm not sure how you can live with a monster and not know it, but this girl is the exception to the rule. You know I've interrogated, questioned and researched much worse characters than Sonja and I'm telling you, she simply doesn't know."

"Fine. Get up there and meet him. Get in his good graces and his bank accounts. I want information and I want it yesterday. That man finances and controls over half the girls taken from the country. No one comes close to him in human trafficking. He doesn't give a crap about anything else. Now we've got to deal with some other mobster trying to pick off his family one by one. Dominik was Hugo's oldest son and his number one guy. He's the youngest person to ever have solid control over that much area of a country. Now he's gone. And don't think that makes your job any easier. Rüdiger may be a year younger but he's much more apt to shoot you where you stand just for trying to step into the family, much less the family business. I don't have much to go on, but rumor is that Rudy actually took a beating for his sister once, and Hugo still doesn't know the whole story. So Rudy may have some sort of sweet spot for his little sister but she's probably the only one."

"What are the chances her mother knows anything?"

"She's a female so chances are about as slim as Sonja's, I guess. He's really the smoothest character I've seen. His restaurant is small and quaint. Good food I hear, and Brigitte keeps her focus on that little shop. If the daughter knows nothing like you say and she's lived with him her entire life, maybe he slipped up somewhere early on and her mother might know something. It's worth a try, but be very careful how you approach it. Remember, to these men, women are nothing."

Chapter 8

Even though Sonja and Danny left at 6 a.m., and took the three-hour flight from Oslo to Hanover, they still didn't arrive at her parent's restaurant until noon. The "closed" sign was still up on the door, but Sonja just turned the knob and Danny followed her right inside. Although the lights were dim, Brigitte knew exactly who had just walked in. Sonja met her mother in the middle of the shop. Rudy stood eyeing Danny as he took his turn hugging his sister.

"Who is your friend?" he asked. Sonja took a step back and felt Danny right by her side. Introductions were made. Danny could see a figure standing in the back of the shop near the waiter serving window. Hugo was cautious of any man he didn't already know as a customer to be stepping into his place, and he considered Danny to be an enemy already. Danny could tell by his body language and the intense eye contact that he was being sized up.

"Hello. I'm Daniel Southerland. I'm a friend of Sonja's," Danny said as he held out his hand. Hugo just stood there. His normal salesman's attitude was gone. He wasn't selling food, his store was closed so this wasn't going to make him any money being nice to some stranger, and he didn't give a damn about any friend of Sonja's.

Brigitte instinctively knew when she needed to leave the room so she grabbed Sonja by the hand. They walked to the stairs, and as Sonja passed Hugo and Rudy, she turned her head and looked over her shoulder at Danny. Her eyes were sad as if she was saying "sorry" but Danny's eyes told her not to worry. Uncomfortable situations were not something where he was afraid of. He actually expected this from Hugo. Danny had already played out in his mind several scenarios of and was prepared for the cold shoulder to a full assault. He watched their every move, especially their hands and eyes. He was looking for anything that would give them away as the true thugs they were.

Hugo sat at a table and motioned for Danny to sit down. Danny grabbed a chair, spun it around and started to sit down, but Rudy stopped him. Danny furrowed his eyebrows as if to wonder what the heck was going on, but he knew. Rudy motioned for him to put his arms out and then proceeded to give Danny a cursory pat down.

"Is this how you say hello in your establishment?" Danny asked as he looked Rudy directly in the eye. "Don't be a smart ass. I don't know why you're here Mr. Southerland. I don't know you. You show up the day after my brother dies and..." Rudy starts to be mouthy but Hugo held his hand up for him to shut up.

"Mr. Southerland. Tell me how you know Sonja and why you're here."

"Sonja didn't tell you?" Danny posed his question carefully.

"No. Unfortunately I have been very busy and Sonja should be studying." Hugo replied as he tilted his head and looked at Daniel.

Daniel was not swayed by Hugo's body language. He proceeded to discuss his love for the arts, travel and how he made money. Daniel dropped subtle hints about money just enough to allow Hugo to be interested. Daniel had studied body language and reactions during his specialized training and could tell by Hugo's micro expressions if he was interested in the subject and decided to wait until Hugo started asking questions. And ask he did.

Hugo was specifically searching by asking very pointed questions. Daniel was more than prepared and even brought Rudy into the conversation to allow him to be a part and get a bit more comfortable with him, too. The three men talked for several hours before the women returned. Sonja looked at Danny and her expression was asking if they could leave. Danny made up some reason to leave and took Sonja by the hand to show everyone that he was now in control of her, and she, of course, was certainly willing to go. Sonja and Brigitte had already discussed their relationship, so Brigitte was fine with Sonja leaving. Moments later they were at their hotel and getting ready for dinner...not at the family restaurant.

The next day was uneventful except for more male dominance in discussing finances. Danny was certainly winning over Rudy while Hugo was still remaining firm and cautious. Danny dropped several small innuendos that he would show Hugo how he can handle his own finances, but would need access to the books. Hugo, always cautious and slow, wasn't taking the bait as fast as Danny would like and was - once again - running into a proverbial brick wall. Hugo continued asking some questions, becoming more interested in Daniel as a person rather than someone who wanted to play with his finances. Daniel acted as if he was an open book and answered as best he could. Sonja and Brigitte cooked in the kitchen just for their men while the shop remained closed until after the funeral the next day. By now the entire neighborhood had heard of Dom's death, and no one bothered them for being closed. Proper etiquette for this neighborhood was three days of mourning, then it was back to business as usual. But there was going to be nothing usual for their last day of mourning.

Chapter 9

She sat quietly in a chair in the corner of the room. The shadows of the room fell gently across her fedora-style hat with a wider brim which blocked the sun from her face. She wore very dark sunglasses and dark red lipstick. Dressed in a ladies business suit which covered her 9mm Glock under her left arm and a personal .380 mm that fit in the small of her back. Her black handbag, mostly just for show for being a "lady", had two throwing knives hidden in the bottom, accessible from under the purse on the outside. Her business suit jacket was tailored just for her and fit perfectly over her pencil skirt. She sat with her legs crossed, the skirt slit showing half her thigh. She wore four-inch stilettos, and her wavy white hair fell gently over her shoulders.

His hand firmly slapped the table just before he pointed in her direction and spoke. "She's done her job. Today," he paused triumphantly, "... they must now bury that boy of his. Then we are going to bury him. Are you ready to do your job?" Nick asked. Nicklaus Don Heinrich III was sitting at the head of the table looking at his comrades. Five rough-looking men sat around the table. All of them grew up in the streets just like Hugo, with one slight exception. Women were a nonperishable product. Unlike Hugo who simply kidnapped them and sold them off as animals, Nicklaus kept them for prostitution. They were property. He even kept a few of the most beautiful as high-end escorts for those who could afford the luxury, and, of course, a couple of them kept him company as well. His client list was a veritable who's who in the corporate business world of this area. A few of them were even politicians who did a few favors every now and then in return for special favors. Nicklaus was, without a doubt, the man who commanded the most respect in this room. The five men who sat in front of him were actually the boss of their own territory, but only because Nicklaus Don Heinrich III allowed them to be, and they knew it.

Nicklaus rose from his chair slowly. He slowly walked around the table, making a speech to these territorial dictators detailing the plan on eliminating Hugo Henie. Nicklaus had had an ax to grind with Hugo for the last seventeen years, only Nicklaus hadn't known who was to blame until recently. Hugo was very quiet about what he did, and he didn't play well with others. He certainly wasn't going to be told what to do.

Nicklaus's reason for revenge sat in the corner of the room wearing red lipstick. Hugo's men had picked her up when she was only 14. She was a small, scrawny thing working the streets, picking up tricks for Nicklaus's own city when she suddenly disappeared. Nicklaus thought she had run away, as some of them try to do. When in actuality, Hugo's men found her strung out in an alley, and thought she would never be missed. And she really wasn't. But growing up in the streets can give you some education you wouldn't get anywhere else. She was an exceptional pick-pocket and thief. Quick and quiet, she could pass the School of the Seven Bells without skipping a beat. Somehow between being tied up, boxed in a train car, and shipped around with eleven other girls of various ages, she was able to untie herself, slip past her guards, and slide away in to the night air. The guards and most of the girls never saw her leave. The two who did told the guards that she ran a different direction than was true, in hopes that she would return with help for them. She never looked back. Those girls knew exactly what they were doing when they started this life, just like she did. She was simply more aware that circumstances can change at any time, but only if you actually do something about them.

She didn't go back to Nicklaus right away. She kept her distance, knowing that they would be looking for a petite brunette with blue eyes by the name of Penny. She knew Penny must vanish. She stole a boat from a nearby dock and drifted out into the cold waters. She smelled horrible and decided to bathe in the river. The water was freezing. A week later and 150 miles down the road she stopped for the night. Hungry, she hid behind a small farm house, digging through the trash when a young boy found her. She was about to run when he offered her food from the main house. Hunger won over her decision to run and she followed the boy into the house. Once his parents saw her, they knew she needed help. They fed her and put her up for the night ever fearful that the man in the house would sneak into her room. She didn't speak to them that night but she couldn't avoid conversation in the morning. She gave them a false name. She watched how the boy and his father treated his mom in a loving, caring manner. Feeling safer than she had in a long time, she kept to herself, helped out where she needed to and ended up staying longer than intended. She did chores to pull her own weight and kept her mouth shut most of the time. Mikhail, the boy who found her, started going back to school when the time came, and she was expected to attend as well. She didn't like it at all, but she didn't have anywhere else to go. She decided to practice her thievery skills right there at school, either on students or teachers and no one ever suspected the cute little shy brunette.

One afternoon on the school grounds she was being picked on by an older boy. He had pushed her to the ground. Standing up for her, Mikhail got in a fight and almost effortlessly beat up the bully. It really wasn't even a fair fight in her eyes. He didn't kick or jump at all but simply maneuvered around, grabbed an arm or a wrist and threw the bully to the ground until he gave up. But her attacker was at least 30 pounds heavier. She was impressed.

On the way home she talked Mikhail into training her to fight for herself. For all the time she spent with them so far, she never knew the boy's family knew martial arts. Several months after she started her training, his father was impressed by her physical skill while still remaining very timid around him. He didn't have any clue about her past but he could tell with some certainty that she had been treated poorly and he was pretty sure it was by a man – maybe several of them. When he tried to come closer she held her hand up in a traditional STOP method and politely asked, "Just show me, please." He complied as always. Her actual hand to hand combat was rigid. She was very self-aware of her surroundings and knew exactly how close he was. He didn't invade her privacy unless she made mistakes in her training and only then she was more upset with herself for the mistake. He remained professional – as did she even at her young age. He respected her personal boundary and knew she was a good student. She picked up on her training quickly so he began to teach her about rifles, pistols, and archery. He taught her about strategy, planning ahead and trying to know your opponent's next steps. She was an exceptional student. They, Mikhail's father and mother, also taught her how to communicate and how to actually carry on a conversation. They hoped she would someday have a conversation with Jesus. In the after-hours of the evening, when training was over and the house was silent, they both prayed for her. She was a lost soul and even when they tried to have a conversation about Jesus Christ, she would not participate. She put her hand up in the STOP position or walked out of the room. Peace or any form of understanding or forgiveness was simply not of interest to her.

Teaching her to converse turned out as her least favorite task. As a quiet, shy girl, she wouldn't get very far in life without talking to people. She excelled at everything she put her mind to. She had plenty of time to think about her life – to plan ahead. With the exception of Mikhail and his father, she hated men in general. She was going to make all the evil men pay for what they had done. Seven years later she showed up at Nicklaus' office.

Nicklaus didn't know who stood in front of him and he didn't care. She was just some scrawny girl with pearl white hair, baggy jeans, and a t-shirt. Nicklaus had no idea how she came to be standing in his doorway, and didn't think too much of it until he called for his men to remove her. The three men stood up and walked toward her. They were about to learn a painful lesson. She was patiently waiting for them to move closer. In two more steps she would start her assault. Without warning, she had kicked the inside of the first guy's right knee, driving him to the ground. She could see his gun in his waistband and rolled over his back while grabbing it. She watched as the two other men followed her motions. Then she spun and slammed the butt of the gun on the bridge of the nose of the closest idiot. He was out like a light. The third guy was drawing his gun when she grabbed the heavy glass ash tray and threw it at his face, hitting him in his right eye. The first idiot was up and coming toward her fast. He tried to draw his gun, not realizing she had taken it. He threw his first punch and she blocked to the outside, side-kicking the inside of his other knee, sending him to the ground again. She kicked away the gun from the second goon who apparently decided it was a good idea to try and get up. She looked at him and shook her head while pointing the gun directly at Nicklaus.

Nicklaus was impressed.

"We need to talk," she said.

"What's your name?" he asked.

"Shut up and listen. When I'm done, you're going to tell me we have a deal." For the past seven years she had been formulating a plan to get revenge. She was starting with Hugo, and Nicklaus was going to help her do it. She outlined how Nicklaus's territory would grow and that she would be able to help with taking care of anyone who got in his way. She would be a phone call away and stay in the shadows. She had already proven she could handle herself, having dispatched three of his men who collectively outweighed her by 40 to 45 kilograms. He would pay her handsomely, and saying no was not an option. Reluctantly, he agreed to her terms.

"What do I call you?" he asked again.

"Luna," she answered. And with that, she ejected the gun's magazine, unchambered the round, detached the slide, and dropped it all on the floor in less than 3 seconds and calmly walked toward the door. Nicklaus opened his top desk drawer and looked down at his gun. Luna's head turned and her eyes fixed upon Nicklaus. His eyes opened wide as he saw the letter opener which was previously been on his desk come flying towards him. It landed just beside the right side of his face, stuck deep into the leather of his chair. She shook her head disapprovingly and left the room.

Patience wasn't her middle name but she was damn good at it. After Luna had "negotiated" with Nicklaus and he had caved, as if he was even given a choice, she fulfilled her threats against the five bosses as promised. They also caved, but some were even more of a challenge than Nicklaus Don Heinrich III. He only had two things that she needed. First, he controlled the territory where Hugo lived. That was more important than the second item he had, which was a feared name. His captains and lieutenants were good enough that they created more of a fear of him than that of the other territorial bosses. She also studied him before she made her move. His organization was well run, but the man himself, when alone and without an audience, could be persuaded. She picked the time and the place and even expected him to have some bodyguards around that she would dispatch just to prove her point and not leave any witnesses other than him. She put the fear of the White Witch in him. As far as he knew, he was the only one who knew her name.

Chapter 10

Over the next year Nicklaus's territory grew. He privately met with each of the five bosses of the territory and made a simple proposition. If they disagreed, and they all did, their muscle would shrink one-by-one until they changed their minds. Every boss had finally heard of the White Witch, obviously due to the color of her hair that Nicklaus had spoken of, but no one had seen her in action as she took out each of their personal body guards. They only saw the bodies fall beside them or found the bodies later. They all thought she was a rumor and Nicklaus was trying to take over their territory. Which wasn't entirely wrong. Nicklaus was taking over. She picked him to do so. If he wanted to live, he didn't really have much of a choice. It was only a matter of time before the rumor had to be addressed.

Finally, a few of the goons she let live realized she was a very bad dream come to life. Leaving them alive and letting them see her helped solidify their fear of her. The sore and beaten men embellished the stories of how she had beaten, tortured, stabbed or shot them, which did everything to help her cause. She counted on that to happen and not one of them let her down. It didn't take long for all of them to swear allegiance to Nicklaus Don Heinrich III as he and he alone had control over the White Witch. She quietly took out anyone who got in the way of her plan, and Nicklaus got the credit. She was number one, but she remained in the background to not bring any attention to herself though everyone felt her presence, until the time was right.

Now she was sitting in the room with the five most respected evil men in the territory, the newly created "board members". And she let Nicklaus be in charge. The corner of the room was covered in shadows yet they could just make out her female form clothed in black, her bright red lipstick, red high heels and wisps of her ghost white hair over her left cheek. She didn't say a word as their eyes casually glanced in her direction. This was the closest they had ever been to the White Witch. Even though the men were powerful businessmen, and they tried not to show it, she could almost smell the fear in the air. She smiled ever so slightly.

"For too long this man, Hugo Heine, has been taking our girls and making them disappear," Nicklaus began. "He's been stealing what rightly fully belongs to us. His whole damn operation is small but very effective. He takes his time with his prey. He's smart. He understands power and all of his goons are fiercely loyal to him. The problem is, he's been infringing on our profits!" Nicklaus slapped his open hand on the table in front of him. "Until recently, no one knew who was he was. Until recently, he was able to work under our noses and embarrass us. Until just yesterday he had two sons. Tomorrow he buries his oldest boy, and he will soon bury the other. Each of you has one day to send us your very best muscle. We have specific needs to complete our task."

Nicklaus had already done some homework, or rather Luna did the work and told Nicklaus what she wanted him to say. Nicklaus pointed to each individual boss and told him who to bring to the next meeting. Two of the bosses acted very shocked that Nicklaus even knew they had such talent, and Nicklaus's eyes tightened just enough to show each man that he knew everything about their operation. Then, to tighten the screws on those who were about to lie to him, he just glanced in her direction. The men's blood nearly turned cold right there as the hair raised on the back of their necks.

The oldest man in the room was running the Northwest Territory. While that area wasn't very large in comparison to others, it held the most coastal property. Therefore, he controlled most of the water transport, essential in some of their operations. He had been in the game for a long time. Even though he wasn't impressed with Nicklaus, he was impressed with her. He was sizing up this conversation for what it truly was. A power play. But whose power? And who was playing whom?

"Nicklaus, "he said cautiously. "If I may..." and he waited for the nod from the head of the table. "I'm wondering what we know of this Hugo character. How has he been able to work in our arena as long as he has without us knowing who he is? Why now? How did he slip up? How did he teach his men to stay clear of our operation? Would we be able to glean any information to make our territory stronger by learning from him? I understand he has disrespected all of us. I do. And I will gladly give you the men you request, but I'd like to know why we kill him now instead of interrogating him so we can prevent this from happening in the future."

The man in the gray suit coat didn't move a muscle as he waited for Nicklaus to answer. He had a point. This had never happened before on a scale such as this and certainly not in an area as large as these territories.

"I'll tell you what you wish to know, Mr. Gruber. It took a long time to research this question you rightly asked. As we didn't know who this man was or even when we would strike, we had to have patience. We studied the types of girls he would take from us. Many of the girls were low-end junkies whom we thought were useless. Some of them we barely even considered as useful. A few of them we got hooked on drugs were so messed up that they took too long to dry out. We waited too long to put them back on the street. We didn't notice them so much since they didn't produce much. Hell, he probably saved us some time and effort of keeping up with the little shits. That's how he started. He capitalized on our own mistakes. Quietly in the alleys, looking for girls behind the bars, beside the dumpsters, passed out in the dark doorways. They probably couldn't even scream when he plucked them from right beneath us. He may have been doing us a favor then by cleaning out our trash. Then he started getting greedy. Better girls. Even some that didn't belong to us. College girls that came from abroad to study here started to go missing. Our own clients began to purchase girls from him. Let's call those 'higher quality'. We started to lose business. That was his first mistake. He drew attention to himself. Rumor has it that the girls started walking in pairs even when we told them to go separately.

They feared going missing more than they feared the back of our hand. He's cunning. But he's overconfident. We now know that he drugged the girls; they were vulnerable and he drove them away silently. He sold them for a profit which should have been ours. We found where he kept the girls down by the docks. A quiet place away from the main shipping channel. His operation is blown. We KNOW how Mr. Gruber."

Nicklaus's voice got a more gruff to press his answer. He let the conversation lapse for a moment, to let it sink in. His voice got a bit quieter as he continued. "He slipped up as our visitor has been watching him for several months without being noticed. You all know she has the skills to find out everything about her prey. We also know that the only people he trusts are his closest family. His two sons and two of his nephews, who are actually on his wife's side, are his captains and lieutenants. No females in his world know what he really does. The women in his life are just to make him appear normal. This is the way he was undetectable for so long. He's a quiet man with a hatred in his heart toward women. He doesn't even care about his own daughter. He trusts only those four men. And now one of them is dead. And what better place to get the rest of them together than a funeral?"

Gruber nodded for the answer Nicklaus gave.

"The rest of your question, Mr. Gruber is how we prevent this from happening again. We will send a message to everyone by taking out his entire family. The churches will be full next week and the only name in the paper will be from the family of Hugo Heine. It will be published for all to see. There will be no question. We will take out his blood line. And you will do exactly as I say."

Nicklaus sat down, letting everyone know that he was done with anyone questioning him. Luna smirked just a bit as she thought to herself ~ Nicklaus was a good boy who did as he was told.

Chapter 11

Nicklaus and Luna sat in his office four days before Dom's funeral and she told him every part of the plan he needed to know. Nicklaus couldn't believe the layers of strategy she was weaving. Secretly, he wished she truly worked for him instead of controlling him. He kept that to himself as he looked for weaknesses in her plan and in herself. He found none in either.

She would take care of the oldest son the following day. That would start a chain reaction to protect the family. First there would have to be a funeral bringing the family members together in a single place. Hugo's operations will shut down for a couple days giving them time to grieve and time for Nicklaus to bring in the hired guns Luna would need to continue. Nicklaus was to call for a meeting with the bosses immediately after killing Dominick. They were to be charged with sending specific shooters and drivers that Luna had already approved. As the bosses were now under Nicklaus's overall command, no one should give them any problems. Clearly, Luna had done her homework.

She noticed the roof and made note of the reinforced roof line that was just about shoulder high and the cutouts that were strategically placed to be used for rifles or other weapons. The front of the restaurant was certainly vulnerable, the best place to attack by surprise. Lots of glass breakage and noise would disorient anyone inside. The attack should last between three to five minutes, giving them time to eliminate all the threats and to get out of the area before the police arrived. She was hoping that she would have witnessed the police response time after killing the oldest son, but since he didn't actually die in the alley, she was using her best guess and could only hope a patrol car wasn't in the area during her attack.

Chapter 12

Daniel sat a few rows behind the family during the funeral. It was an average-sized church and a nice funeral, as far as funerals go. When it was over, the family drove out to the gravesite for the final burial. They didn't stay long. Hugo was of the mind to bury the dead and move on. He also figured Gitta would grieve no matter how long they stayed so they may as well make this short. Not wanting to butt into the family at a public setting, Daniel stayed by the car and watched in silence while the priest performed the ceremony. Sonja cried for a bit but was more saddened for her mother, who was crying most of all. Dominick was an ass to her but he was still her brother. Hugo stood in silence like a statue. Rudy stood right beside, though his eyes watered a bit. His oldest brother was his best friend. As the ceremony concluded, Brigitte grabbed a white rose from off the casket. Hugo placed his hand on the casket for a moment. He seemed to take a deep breath and hold it just for a second before slowly letting it out. Then he turned and walked away toward the car. Brigitte was slightly surprised for him to show any signs of weakness or emotion such as this. Her ice cold blue eyes sitting across the graveyard smiled at this moment.

Daniel opened the car doors for the family as they got into the limousine. The windows were very dark and the family rode home in silence. Daniel followed in his own car. Luna's small black four-door sedan was parked across the cemetery. She watched their every move. Luna wondered who the big man was in the dark gray suit. New hired muscle? She didn't see him the other day during the shooting, hadn't heard about him from any of her organization, and she didn't recognize him as part of the family. She paused for a moment, then decided he was about to be a simple casualty, not giving him a second thought.

It's somehow a world-wide tradition to feed the whole family after a funeral, and what better place than your own restaurant. Brigitte grabbed Sonja by the hand, and with the tears still streaming, Brigitte began cooking. Sonja helped and knew exactly what to do without asking. Hugo was about to put on his own apron when Brigitte just threw out her hands making him leave the kitchen. Today, he knew to leave her to herself and he obliged. Hugo returned to the table where Rudy, Daniel and a few other cousins sat chatting. Some of the cousins were telling stories about Dom. A few of them knew the family business but most of them just knew about the restaurant. Since the store had been closed for several days, it took a little longer to prepare lunch. Only a few entrées were made and Brigitte didn't ask anyone what they wanted. She fixed everything family-style and planned on just setting it all on the table. The food was coming out of the kitchen and smelled scrumptious. Brigitte and Sonja were carrying out several dishes on large trays and setting everything around on several tables. Many of the dishes were al-dente' so everyone could share 'family style'. She was feeding about fifteen to twenty people. The conversation was humming and there was nothing quiet about it. The large group was always loud when they got together and this was no exception.

Daniel knew that time was important and he needed to begin his mission. He sat chatting with family members, waiting until Hugo's mind wandered back to money. It didn't take long. Some of the family began saying their goodbyes, and somewhere around three o'clock Hugo's employees started calling to see if they were going to work tonight for the dinner run. The restaurant was open and they needed to work to get paid. Those questions helped churn Hugo's mind to thinking about the restaurant. He had already begun to plan a strategy to find out who killed Dom. He remembered glancing at the rooftop as they came back from the gravesite and could barely make out that the team was still in place. Hugo looked over at Daniel and motioned for him to come sit closer. Daniel calmly excused himself from the conversation with one of the last cousins to hang around and grabbed a chair to casually sit next to Sonja's father.

Hugo didn't much like the man sitting as close as he did. He was still practically a stranger and there was just the two of them at the four-top table. He should have sat across from him. Hugo eyed him sternly but Daniel didn't back down. Daniel could tell sitting so close made Hugo slightly uncomfortable, which was his intent. He needed Hugo to be a bit off guard. He also wanted to be able to lean in and speak in hushed tones. Hugo would have to listen more carefully and concentrate on what Daniel said. He also knew that this would put the women in the room out of the conversation, making Hugo respect him in his own way. Daniel knew he would end up guiding Hugo right where he wanted him. And that's exactly what he did. Their conversation lasted for over an hour, with Daniel creating a web of information that was more than college-level finance. Hugo was liking what he heard. Hugo began asking the leading questions that were nearly always followed by statements such as, "When can we start?" It was then that Daniel knew he just won this volley, but his satisfaction would have to wait as the front door glass was shattered by the firing of semi-automatic weapons.

Luna had watched Hugo Henie leave his dead son's funeral and the gravesite. She had tracked his moves for the last three days and patiently waited for the moment to strike. She was about to send him a message he wouldn't soon forget. She planned to take everything away from him. She wanted him to do something he had never done before. She wanted to make him beg.

She called her small team together about noon and went over the plan. Her team consisted of the best muscle from each of the mobs represented at the table three days before. They didn't like giving up their own body guards but she had already convinced each mob boss that they would cooperate. She very explicitly gave each man certain instructions. She wanted this to go off like clockwork, but since these goons hadn't ever worked together before, she wasn't sure how they would react. They were used to actually working against each other. Each of their own bosses had charged them to take care of issues against each other and here she is making them work together. It was a dangerous cocktail she was playing with, but on short notice it was her best option. She did not carry the old Arabic proverb of "The enemy of mine enemy is my friend." That friend stuff was bullshit. An enemy is just that, an enemy. She thought it should have been stated, "The enemy of mine enemy is an enemy I can use against the other." It keeps them all in the right perspective. No friends. Period. And the time to start eliminating her enemy was getting closer.

She deployed her team and gave them plenty of time to get into place. Two of them were several blocks away. The others were just down the street from the restaurant where food and stories were keeping them busy. A few of the extended family were starting to leave but those were Brigitte's second or third cousins and no one of consequence. She waited a bit longer and gave the sign.

The rooftop protection detail Hugo had placed was standing at the ready. They were watching each street, believing that nobody knew they were up there, until a bullet pinged off the corner of the roof. Each of the four men instantly alerted, dropping below the roofline trying to determine where it came from. The second bullet caused a pink spray to pop from the side of one of the guard's head. He fell lifeless on the rooftop. The sniper was above them! How the hell anyone knew they were up there was pissing them off. They ran to the opposite roofline and shoved their rifles in the cutouts, looking through their scopes for the sniper. That was where she wanted them. Her second sniper was perched within another building two blocks away, one floor above. Focused on one at a time, he fired his first shot hitting his mark in the base of the neck of the second guard. He fired his second shot just a second later, hitting the third guard in the right side of his chest as he tried to move for cover. He was unable to put the crosshairs of his Leupold scope on the third guard in time. The captain of the guard grabbed his teammate and dragged him behind the iron cover as quickly as he could. He was furious that they were all sitting ducks. Somehow, someone got the better of them. It didn't take him long to hear the sounds of bullets flying from the streets below.

Each member of the three-man walking team was armed with a Beretta M1951 and carried two extra magazines in their shoulder holsters. As the restaurant was on the corner, Luna had each man pick a street and casually walk toward Hugo's Restaurant. Coming from streets directly across from the front door, the two of them watched as a few people exited the establishment. When they heard the first shot coming from the roof, they knew it was time to start killing. Their orders were to kill anyone left inside. Elimination without reservation. Just as one of them stepped to cross the street, Rudy saw it. "GUN!" he yelled.

Brigitte and Sonja were still clearing dishes from the tables when the first shot crashed through the front door. Both of them screamed and brought their shoulders up and threw their hands in their faces. Daniel's training kicked into high gear but he couldn't give himself away just yet. Hugo quickly jumped behind the front counter and grabbed a shotgun and threw it to Rudy. He grabbed his own pistol and they both began returning fire. The two gunmen used the cars outside as cover but were slowly working their way closer. Tables were being thrown over for cover as bullets continued to come through the door. Pictures shattered and holes were dotting the walls. Daniel could tell it was small arms fire, but there was no way to know how many rounds they could have with them or even how many shooters there were. He glanced at a clock noticing the time. This couldn't last more than five minutes like this. Somebody will call the police. Daniel pushed Sonja and Brigitte into the kitchen and made sure the back door was bolted. The ladies continued to scream and other family members were ducking behind anything they could find. Bodies fell as the bullets found their mark; blood was filling the floors. Daniel noted that Rudy's pump shotgun had just emptied and he was reloading. Daniel was already returning up front to join the fight as one of the shooters stepped out from behind the car, staring at Rudy. Running past Rudy, trying to draw the fire his way, Daniel grabbed a solid glass ashtray from a table and hurled it full force and connected with the shooter's face throwing him into a daze just long enough for

Rudy to fire a hip shot into the gut of the shooter. Daniel rolled behind a table and acted surprised.

Above them on the roof, the captain checked the wound of his remaining partner. The bullet slammed into the iron inserts of his body armor and took the breath out of him while breaking several ribs. The captain ran to the center of the roof to the munitions boxes, drawing the fire from the sniper. Just as he dove behind, he saw what he needed. He threw his body into a very low shoulder roll then immediately into a kneeling position, aimed his FAL and began to let every round into the direction of the sniper. He was expecting to hear bullets from the other direction but it didn't come. He also noticed that he wasn't being fired upon any more. Running over to the edge of the building he was able to see one shooter's head jerk back from a large glass object being thrown and then his whole body pushed back as he was hit with a shotgun blast. Making a quick assessment, he could see one gunman on the right firing into the restaurant and he noticed a third crouching behind a car down to his left. He drew his Phantom from its holster and let loose on him. The gunman was pinned down with no help in sight. Hugo noticed the car across the street was being shot at and could only assume it was from the roof, though he wondered why it was small arms fire and not the FAL shredding the car.

Daniel couldn't help but engage in the battle, but he couldn't draw his own weapon so he decided to use everything and anything else. They were about two minutes into this crap, and he didn't have much time left. The tables wouldn't last much longer for cover. Apparently, the gunmen had more clips or there were more shooters than he could see.

The captain noticed his last partner had just worked his way up beside him and pointed his FAL down toward the street to begin raining fire down below, until he suddenly slumped. His FAL fell down and landed in the broken glass in front of the restaurant. The first sniper must have repositioned himself. The captain saw the muzzle fire coming from the street level about two hundred yards ahead.

Thinking he could now run around the roof safely, he retrieved his own FAL, reloaded, grabbed two more magazines, and began hailing bullets in that direction. The sniper only needed one shot to finish him.

Hugo looked at Daniel as he reloaded his last magazine into his pistol. Both of them knew the gunman across the street would stand up any second and begin his assault. No one was shooting in his direction now. Rudy was out of shells and this was about to get really nasty. Daniel watched as his luck fell from the sky. He recognized the FAL as it fell and rushed outside. He grabbed the FAL and pointed it toward the closest target, watching as that gunman went down fast and ugly. As soon as the bullet connected with his first target, his eyes were locked on the second. He spun the FAL toward the car - the last gunman. Keeping his eyes trained directly on him, when the muzzle was close he pulled the trigger and caught him in the chest several times. Then he sprayed another ten or fifteen rounds in the neighborhood and acted shocked that he could have even hit the broad side of the barn. Hugo and Rudy starred at him for a moment until the sniper down the street put a bullet right by Hugo's head, barely missing him. Hugo ducked behind the closet car with its lights blinking and alarm cranking out some sickly beeping sounds. Rudy ran towards his dad, but Daniel knocked him to the ground as more shots pinged off the car and walls nearby. Daniel couldn't see the exact point where this shooter was hiding until he saw powder coming off the walls. He heard the rounds coming from above. He looked up and saw the front of another FAL and he was thankful is wasn't pointed in his direction. Hugo yelled up to the roof and the captain could hear the instructions not to let him get away.

While Daniel didn't know who was on the roof, it was evident that Hugo did. Daniel was watching the powder come off the walls. He could also hear sirens in the background coming in fast. Daniel decided it was time for a little football action. Crouched down where Hugo couldn't see, he dropped the FAL and picked up a Beretta, checked the magazine, counted the bullets and chambered a round, looked up at the man with the matching FAL and ran in the direction of the sniper at full speed. He loved to run. He zigged in and out from between the cars trying to draw out the sniper to give up his position in hopes the man on the roof wouldn't shoot him and would be able to get a good shot off and kill the sniper. Hugo could see his plan as soon as he started running so he yelled for a little cover fire. The sniper took the bait and began to follow Daniel left and right, left and right, in and around the parked cars. Daniel stuttered his speed so he wouldn't be such an easy target to follow. Daniel was getting closer, and the sniper kept thinking this man was an idiot who was asking to die. The sniper stood in the doorway just far enough out where the captain locked on to him. The captain slowly pulled the trigger when he felt a thud in his back and pain in his chest. He looked down to saw a barbed arrow sticking through his chest. Luna's talents knew no bounds. She was silent and obviously deadly. She slowly walked to the edge of the roof to watch the end of this skirmish. The shot the captain just fired missed the sniper, causing him to look up at the roof just long enough for Daniel to fire all the shots into the doorway. The first round killed the sniper as the bullet pierced his neck. The other bullets were all for effect. Daniel quickly wiped the weapon and through it down the alley. As he slowly walked back to the restaurant with sweat dripping off his face, blood spots coming through his shirt from landing and rolling on broken glass, he could see someone on the roofline. A female with very white hair was staring back at him.

Chapter 13

"Who the hell are you?" Hugo yelled at Daniel. Daniel had formulated an answer to several questions while the blood was still a bit damp on his shirt. His response had to be full of testosterone for Rudy, while pretty much void of emotion for Hugo, and still remain true to Sonja. He wasn't sure how he should formulate an answer if Brigitte was involved. She hadn't said much to him yet.

"From the looks of it, I'm the man who saved your ass!"

"Where the hell did you learn that stuff?" Rüdiger asked, as if he could tell he had training.

"Stuff! You mean where did I learn to run? I played football back in the U.S.! Where did I learn to shoot? I can't! I saw that damn thing and just pointed and pulled the trigger. Not to mention I did it at the time when you ran out of bullets, you prick. And you!" he eyed Hugo dead on and stepped toward him for the ungrateful man he really was, "You, I pushed out of the way when Mr. Bullets down the street was trying to mow you down and all you wanted to do was let the man do it! No, you don't HAVE to say 'Thanks' but it sure wouldn't hurt, asshole." Hugo stood stone-faced.

Tears in her eyes and still recovering from shock, Sonja stepped toward Daniel and grabbed his arm with both of her arms and stood boldly by the man she loved with a bit of something in her stance that resembled defiance against her father. Brigitte walked passed them both and looked at Hugo. She had never done anything like this before. She had always turned away, looked the other way or even took the back of his hand across her face if she couldn't move away quickly enough. Somehow, this matter seemed to be a bit different. There were witnesses now. Her son, her daughter and only a few family members who survived this ordeal. Then this stranger who seemed to save the day in some way. This man that rushed into the face of evil without fear but only did so because it was the right thing to do. Somehow she felt he would step right into Hugo if he tried anything stupid at this point.

"Hugo. This man just saved us! All of us that he could." She waived her hands toward the floor where bodies were still lying around. "He fought by your side, Hugo. He saved Rudy. He saved Sonja and me. And he pushed you out of danger too, Hugo. He saved you, too. Why would this man do this thing? Think about that Hugo. I think he loves Sonja. A man who loves her like this," she said slowly waving her arms around this unholy bloody show, "like this Hugo...to save a family he does not know....is a man among men." She didn't dare take any of this fight away from him. Hugo was a man who simply would not bend his pride for anyone.

"Father," Rudy said gently. "We don't really know this man, but for this day. But if there was any day to know him, today is most definitely the day." Rudy very calmly walked over and put his right hand on Daniel's shoulder and nodded very thankfully as he looked toward his father.

Rudy walked over to his father and whispered something only he could hear. "He plays with money. He obviously doesn't play with guns. Maybe we could teach each other something someday?"

Hugo looked at his son Rüdiger as he tried to come to grips with what just happened. Was this man a mole from the enemy? He quickly ruled out this option. The other men were too well prepared and this man had no weapons. Hugo took a slow, deep breath while the remaining family retreated to the back of the building. Sonja and her mother sat crying, still in disbelief. Hugo finally turned to Daniel who had sat down in a chair about five feet away. Hugo took two steps toward Daniel, still holding the pistol in his right hand. He looked down at Daniel, speaking sternly. "Daniel. In moments like these I'm not a man of many words." He said as he slowly raised his right hand. He still had his finger on the trigger. Daniel looked right back into the eyes of Hugo and watched as Hugo handed the pistol to Rudy. Then he extended his arm with his opened hand. Daniel stood slowly and grasped Hugo's hand in a firm handshake. Hugo nodded his approval.

After she left the rooftop perch, witnessing at the stranger, she went directly to Nicklaus and told him what just happened. While Nicklaus was furious from losing some of the best men in all the territories, he was more enraged that Luna's plan failed. What he really wanted to do was come across the table and throat punch her, but he also knew she was too fast for him and she might possibly injure himself for life. She wouldn't kill him. She still needed him, they had both agreed that this wasn't over yet. She didn't have a backup plan just yet, but she would, and for that, she was going to disappear for a while.

"What do you expect me to tell the board members?" he asked.

"I suggest you grow a pair and start acting like you're in charge. If it was me, I'd blame someone else."

"Someone else? They're all dead. I can't blame the incompetence of a dead man. That just leads to the others thinking they must take the blame since it was their man. And those men were really good, Luna."

"I don't mean blame your own organization, you dolt! Blame Hugo's new man. The man in the gray suit. Somehow he didn't fit into our equation and it cost us today's win. It's like a chess game, Nicklaus. The board is something we must look very carefully at before making our move. Today we used a few bishops to take out some of their pawns and a few knights off the roof. However, their King was ready. He is no fool, Nicklaus. He had a rook in waiting and it was devastating to us. We didn't see him. It's our fault for not knowing anything about him and for underestimating his worth."

"And you, my queen. You were there. The most powerful player in chess." He looked carefully at Luna while saying this. His heart skipped a beat when he realized he just spoke out loud.

Her ice blue eyes turned in his direction when she replied, "Yes, and knowing when to retreat is just as important as knowing when to regroup. I told you this was my mistake. It will not happen again. Now, let's go over what you will do now. I will be leaving for a while to do what I must. Hugo is not a stupid man. He will prepare differently and he will be ready for us."

"When will I know that you have a new plan?"

"You'll know when you need to."

"How do I contact you?"

"You don't." With that said, she left.

Nicklaus called the board members, described the man in the gray suit and blamed the day's loss on him.

Chapter 14

Several miles away she drove her little black car with the window down. She was pissed that she under estimated this new man. Her research found nothing about him. Some stupid man selling financial wealth information was all she could find. This lucky bastard tore her plans all to shreds and she knew nothing about him. Plans could be remade, but poor planning was no excuse. She should have thought about the unknowns, maybe used more men, and tried the attack earlier, or even at night. She was so frustrated she couldn't think straight. She just drove her sedan as fast as she dared. She kept the driver's window open and let the breeze blow her white hair. The only consolation she had was that not a single member of her team survived. If they had, she would have killed them herself.

Vowing that this wasn't over, she drove several hours and fumed over her failure. Hugo and his family were to be dead by now. All of them. He did this to her and he was going to pay the ultimate price. Rage continued to build up in her until she screamed as loud as she could and slammed her fist into the dashboard. She drove until she finally stopped at the docks. Her 38' sport yacht was waiting for her. Well, it wasn't actually hers, but it was now. It was quiet, dark and peaceful. She stepped on board and went below deck and popped open a bottle of Bordeaux. The night air was crisp and she welcomed it to clear her head of emotions. She needed to think clearly and methodically in order to plan her next move. She slowly drank her first glass of wine, then filled her glass again. Walking around the deck, she familiarized herself with the plush watercraft. She thought of what went wrong and the only kink in her plan was this stranger. He was fast, but he appeared clumsy when firing a weapon. Somehow he always found his target, though. Something wasn't right about him.

She walked up to the deck and started the boat's engine. She walked back down around port side and cleared all the lines, slowly guiding the boat out of the slip toward open waters. There was no one around to question her actions. She maneuvered the boat about ten miles down the coast and anchored in small, quiet cove. She shed her clothes, dove off the back and swam for about thirty minutes. The water was quite cold now, but she needed to bring her temper down and this was the best way she knew how. Cold water. The colder the better sometimes. She climbed back on board the boat, grabbed a towel and stood in the night air. She had done this before many years ago. Frustrated, angry and ready to tear apart the world for revenge, she stole a small boat. When she was safely away from people she dove overboard. She dove as far down as she could until she thought her lungs would burst, then she slowly let out the oxygen in her lungs and hovered there. She couldn't see anything in the deep darks waters of the night. As she slowly surfaced, she looked around. The only friend she could see was starring right back at her. The moon was so very bright in the cloudless sky. It was there that Penny was no more and Luna came to life.

She stepped back into the yacht, turned on some lights and stepped downstairs to the shower. She was fine now. The cold water had done its job again, and she was ready to plan her next move. She had homework to do.

Chapter 15

Daniel obviously knew that Hugo had fire power on the roof. This was something Brigitte still didn't know about as she was indoors for the entire firefight. As far as Brigitte goes, Hugo simply blew off the attack as some Mafioso gang trying to take his restaurant or property. She didn't really believe him, but she also knew she would probably never know the truth. Daniel and Rudy were the only two Hugo allowed up on the roof. They cleaned the roof, got rid of the bodies and hid them from the police, who also chalked this up to local gang violence.

Once everything was cleaned, Daniel took Sonja by the hand, led her past Hugo to the front door. Daniel turned to Brigitte and gave her a hug. He looked at Rudy and nodded his head, who reciprocated the gesture. "We will return tomorrow." He said as he looked at Hugo. Sonja's father looked at her in a way he had never done. He accepted her decision in the man she was leaving with. He didn't know much about him yet, but vowed he would. He had resources. Hugo nodded and said, "We have much to discuss." With that, Daniel had done accomplished his purpose. He gained Hugo's trust. He didn't know it would take a gun battle to do it!

Daniel didn't go back to the hotel directly. He drove around for over an hour on the outskirts of town and down some very picturesque roads. He and Sonja were both still covered in the mess from earlier. They stopped and cleaned up as best they could. Then Daniel took her out and bought her all new clothes. She deserved it. He bought himself a new suit. While Sonja was trying on new outfits - something she wasn't accustomed to - Daniel called Stack.

"You really know how to make an entrance, Danny." Stack chided him and was also a bit miffed.

"Next time you send me into the Den of Thieves, you should just be prepared to send in a few body bags. Actually, this time was a case of you were right. Someone was planning on killing off more of the family. I really think they were gunning for Hugo Heine himself, or at least his other son. And if it was just Rüdiger, then they are trying to make him suffer. This felt like revenge to me, not just some gangland-style hit. They were prepared. Tactical gear and nice weaponry. Apparently, Hugo was prepared, too. He had four shooters on the roof loaded with FALs and plenty of rounds. But they were taken out first or, at least tried to. The last guy on the roof almost had a bead on me when Hugo told him not to shoot me. He kept the last sniper busy until I popped him. Who the hell is doing this Stack?"

"We're not sure yet, but we think Nicklaus Don Heinrich III is the main character. Hugo has been plucking his girls for over ten years and selling them to the highest bidder. Did you see anything there that would lead you to think otherwise?"

"Just the scariest thing I've seen in my career to date, Stack. I'm not sure if I really saw what I thought I saw."

"Spill it Danny. I don't have all day."

"Well, hold on to your comic book mentality, but listen to this. As soon as I popped the last sniper, I spun around to see the shooter on the roof was slumped over. At the time I couldn't tell why. I was too far away. But I know I saw a female standing over him. When I say over him I mean taller than everything on the roof. She was dressed all in black and had very white hair. That's weird enough but later on when I got to the roof, two things really stuck out. The roof was built so that if you're standing flat foot on the roof itself, you can shoot from the cutouts at shoulder high. But she had moved all the dead bodies and stacked them. When I saw her, she must have been standing on them. Her waist was about as high as the cutouts. She wasn't hiding. She wanted me to see her, Stack."

"Why you?"

"Good question. I've no answer on that."

"You said two things."

"Yeah. The last shooter on the roof was shot in the back of the neck."

"Not so uncommon, Danny. Why is this important?"

"Because I shot him in the shoulder with a bullet. That didn't kill him. He was shot with a barbed arrow, Stack. She was hunting...in the city."

"I think she sent you a message."

Chapter 16

Daniel had just finished talking to his 'corporate office' when Sonja came out of the dressing room. She looked like a hot mess. She was still uneasy about the events of today. He could see it in her eyes. She may have put on clean clothes, but she was quite traumatized. He was hoping the drive in the countryside would help ease her shock. He would also be able to tell if anyone was following him. Or more likely, her. He hadn't seen anything that would make him believe anyone was following either of them. Stack had already agreed to have someone move them from one hotel to another under an assumed name. Sonja didn't know where they were staying anyway.

"You were quite impressive today, Danny. How the heck did you do all that?"

"I don't know, baby. I know when I was a kid, I had always thought of being a cop or the good guy. What little boy doesn't think about that with shows like Batman and Robin or The Lone Ranger, but I never thought I'd have to live it. I'm not even sure you would know who those guys are living here in Europe, but to me, it means I just want to help people."

He answered as best he could while not telling her everything. Deflecting the conversation, he asked, "I'm truly sorry about more of your family passing away. Who was that and what was it all about?"

"I've no idea. My father always seemed to think he owned the best corner lot in all the neighborhood since we did such good business feeding people. He always kept those guns there thinking we might get robbed, but today was a whole lot more than that, obviously. Do you think somebody could be trying to drive him out of the restaurant business?"

"I don't know. They sure had a lot of guns, that's for sure."

"My mother must be totally going crazy right now. Dom just got buried and now we've got more funerals to go to. Her family will be really pissed, too. They were all her family. My father doesn't have anyone else but momma and us kids. Well, Rudy and I."

"And how do you think Rudy is? Is he going to be getting revenge on these people? Does he know who they are?"

"I really don't know, Danny. Once I left I never looked back. You know I was just raised in the kitchen and the ballet studio. When I left, I really didn't expect I'd be back this soon. I thought I'd have another ten years before I had to return, and even then I thought it would be one of my parents' funerals, not Dominick's."

"I don't mean this rudely, Sonja, but it almost was your parent's funeral today. Yours and mine, too!"

She was quiet for a while. She looked at Danny and reached over to the console, taking his hand. She was embarrassed, scared and wondering how they would get through this. She had so many questions in her mind. She stayed focused and calmed herself.

"I'm sorry this happened during your first time meeting my family. But I must say you did save the day!"

"I'm glad I was there to help, if you call falling down and running scared helping." Again answering and then changing the subject.

They continued to drive through the countryside for some time. They both enjoyed the sights and sounds with the sunlight streaming through the trees that covered the roads. Sonja began to notice there were several places she had already seen and asked Daniel if he knew where he was going. Of course he did, and he explained that had played this driving game his whole life. Learning where he was and how to get to a safe place from any direction. It was a game his grandfather taught him a long time ago. In reality, he was making sure they weren't being followed. They finally went to the hotel. Sonja really needed to sleep off the shock of the day. Danny checked in by himself and took Sonja up to the room. He checked in with his boss and found nothing new. He sat on the bed side, watching Sonja fall asleep while his mind kept rehashing the scene of the woman with the white hair. He had no clue who she was, but he was sure of one thing - she was evil, smart, fast, trained and talented. She was a dangerous White Witch.

Chapter 17

They stayed for the weekend. Daniel pumped Hugo about the financial industry and how to use his money in ways he didn't understand. He actually listened this time, a bit more persuaded than before. He wasn't searched for weapons anymore. They at least trusted him that much and conversations were just a bit easier. Hugo was still his staunch and rigid self toward Sonja, but to Daniel, he listened. The remainder of the weekend was cleaning up the store, repairing damaged walls, and feeding the police who stayed in the neighborhood due to the incident. As far as the police knew, this was an attack on a small shop owner. He had the shop looking better than it was in just under a week. He had connections everywhere.

Daniel took Sonja back to Oslo before her next show. Brigitte was sad to see her go, but said she understood if she didn't come back for the other family members' funerals. Most of them wouldn't be in this town anyway. Her performances were still spot on, and she was grateful that she didn't have any bruises showing on her legs and arms from the attack. She was very happy that Danny thought of her first in keeping away from the chaos.

Sonja's performances were getting fantastic reviews. The theatre was doing very well. The theatre owners were even able to do some remodeling since all her performances were nearly sold out. She was a bit exhausted, but in such a good way. She had articles written about her in the paper that she and Danny clipped out and put in small binder she called Things I've Accomplished.

One evening a few weeks after the attack, she had the evening off. Daniel had been away most of the day and she planned something very special. She had wanted to tell him how she felt about him for a long time. She was most definitely in love with him, and she was sure he felt the same, but neither of them had really broached the subject. It felt right without saying it, but something like this was meant to be said. She had gone to the local coffee shop early that morning and met with a friend. Liza and Sonja were like giddy school girls talking about the crush they had on the cute boys they dated. They laughed and giggled for an hour, leaving just in time to start shopping. The women went to several dress shops, with both trying on new clothes. They tried on black, white, with and without camisoles. They tried on long blue and short blue, different shades of orange and a few green. And, of course, they tried on red. A nice fitting red dress cut just above the knee, but still had a small slit up the right leg and a low cut neckline, just enough to let her new heart-shaped pendant fall into her cleavage. Her earrings were almost a perfect match. They weren't real diamonds, but he wouldn't notice, would he? Liza picked out her own dress for her own reasons and the two of them were ready for lunch.

The Engebret Café is one of the oldest restaurants in one of the oldest buildings on Bankplassen, which is more like a picturesque square. A large community square made with brick pavers on the ground laid out in a beautiful array, with a water fountain centerpiece surrounded by park benches, colorful flowers and beautiful trees. It is truly a beautiful place. On the corner is the Engebret Café.

They walked into the elegant building, which was built in the Eighteen Century, sitting down at a table covered with white linen. They ordered a traditional Norwegian meal, and continued to be excited about the new clothes and for her feelings for Danny. Liza was great company who happened to have great taste in clothing, especially as she reminded Sonja the ensemble wasn't complete without shoes!

Just a few blocks away they found the perfect pair of red heels for her dress and her beautifully planned evening. She and Liza parted ways, deciding to meet each other the next day to cover all the details that would transpire that tonight. Sonja stopped at the local market to pick up several items for a homemade dinner. She didn't slave in the kitchen, but made a simple dinner while drinking a glass of wine. She was quite relaxed and was equally anxious to see Danny.

He walked in and she played it very cool. She was still in the kitchen, wearing an apron over her new red outfit. She smiled over her shoulder and could tell he was impressed with the slit down the back. He eyed her from head to toe. She removed the apron, gently laid it on the small kitchen counter and raised her hands, palms out to her side as if to say, "See my new outfit. This is all for you, my love." Her motions didn't go unnoticed on his trained eye. Daniel, the ever so congenial gentlemen, took off his suit jacket and threw it over his shoulder and took a GQ style stance, returning her gestures and saying, "You're in charge tonight. I'm all yours."

"You," he said in low tones, "You are absolutely stunning in red. New shoes, new dress, new necklace and those earrings are strikingly beautiful!"

She blushed a bit as she thought he figured out those weren't really diamonds. She tried to play coy, but she simply couldn't wait. They met each other exactly half way and embraced each other in the most comfortable and warm embrace either of them ever had. She was quite content right there, standing in his arms, when she remembered she was on a mission.

"Dinner smells lovely," he said as she led him to the table. "Please, allow me," he continued as he pulled out one of the two chairs she had in her small apartment. The other chair looked so wonderful with her man sitting in it. That chair he was sitting in used to be depressingly empty as she used to dream of the man who would one day be sitting there across from her. He looked at the stove and could see everything as it should be at the table. She had suddenly forgotten that she was the hostess, and tried to get up to serve him but he wouldn't have it. "Sit. Sit," he said as she blushed again. "I'm here for you. You did all this for us tonight, so please, let me serve you."

"I did this for you, Danny. I should be the one serving you."

"I think I like it this way. You look fantastic. The food smells fantastic. And I think you deserve to be looked after, too."

"Wow," she thought. Is this a dream? Do men really react like this?

"Holy crap!" he thought. I couldn't have picked a more beautiful woman. She loves the ballet. Hell! She's the star of the ballet! She dresses up better than any runway model. She cooks, she's smart, and carries on great conversation. How did I get so lucky? I certainly don't deserve this lot in life, but I do thank God he has blessed me with her.

He served dinner as they ate with light conversation. He made up some story of an easy business day and she told him about her day with Liza. She mixed in a little white lie that today was all about Liza and she just couldn't help herself when they were shopping. That's when she knew it was time to tell him.

"Danny."

"Yes, my dear."

"I need to tell you something. I've been wanting to tell you for a long time, but I really just wanted to be sure."

"Sure, about what?"

"About us."

"And what about us? You are happy, aren't you?" Danny said with a small frown in his brow.

"Yes! I'm the happiest girl in all of Oslo. I wanted to tell you that I'm truly the happiest girl in all of Norway and....and...." she paused as her heart raced, "and I'm in love with the man who gave me roses the first night we met."

"Oh, I see. And is this man handsome? Do I know this stranger?" He played with his words and made her smile.

"Yes. I think you might know him. He's not too tall but still a bit taller than me. He's very handsome. I think you'd like him, too. He's funny, smart and has a wonderful smile. He makes me laugh every day. I couldn't imagine him not knowing how much in love with him I am."

"And is he in love with you?"

"I believe he is. I mean, I really hope he is. Love isn't all it can be unless it's given back to you. And I want to give all of my love to him."

"Sonja," he said in a very serious tone and stood up. He gently took hold of her hand and she stood up, pressing herself up against his chest. He wrapped his arms around her again. "I've been in love with you since the moment I saw you. And I've been wanting to tell you for what feels like the longest time."

"Danny! I love you, too!" she said as she fell deeper into his arms. They kissed and held each other for quite some time when she finally let him go. She looked at the bedroom door and then took his hand and led him to the couch where they both sat down. She could feel her heart beating faster. She knew the moment had come.

"Danny. I'm so very much in love with you. And I want you to know everything about me."

"Good. I want to know everything there is to know."

"Okay. The first thing on my mind that you should know about me is this. I'm about to be a mother."

Danny smiled very big and he pointed at his chest with his index finger. "And I'm about to be a daddy!" It was a statement of fact, not a question. He was obviously overjoyed with her statement and she shook her nodded very emphatically. "Yes!"

He hugged her again and kissed her all over her face and she couldn't stop kissing him back. This couldn't be a more perfect evening.

Danny was kissing her face, then worked his way down her neck spending several minutes there until he ended up on his knees on the floor in front of her.

"Sonja, my love. I do so love you. And you've just made me a very happy man. Do you think…" he paused and grabbed both of her hands. "Could you imagine…" he really wanted to get this right. "Sonja, would you please spend the rest of our lives together being my wife?" he asked as he pulled a ring from his pocket.

Her body shuddered as she gasped for her next breath of air. "Yes! Yes of course!" and he placed the diamond on her finger. She leaned forward and grabbed him to pull him close. She was absolutely elated as she hugged him so hard he could barely breathe, relishing the moment.

The two of them spent the next hour on the couch continuing to make each other lose their breath only to rejuvenate and then make love again. They finally decided to take a break and shower, but they ended up making love there, too. They stepped out of the shower and dried off, returning to bed and holding each other. She was ever so content just lying there in his arms and admiring the ring on her finger.

"Why today?" She asked.

"Why what today?"

"Why did you ask me today? I was trying to surprise you!" She stated, as if he somehow knew this.

"My grandfather once told me that if I were to ever find the girl of my dreams, I should mark it on a calendar. From that day I should wait until I simply couldn't stand it any longer and that's the day I should ask her to marry me. Today is that day and I'm the luckiest man in Norway."

"When did you mark your calendar?"

"I told you, silly. The day we met."

come out soon, she would know this new husband was more than what he appeared. He may be saving his wife, but he was interfering with her plans. This was the second time! She wasn't going to stand for that again. On the other hand, this was getting to be more of a challenge and she did like challenges. Her strategy had to change due to the talents of this man. It must be talent as no one could have this much luck. It was time to focus on the easy targets now and take her time with the professional.

Two blocks away, Daniel sat Sonja on the edge of a bed. She was sitting there in a state of confusion, trying to figure out what just happened. Daniel was standing in the window just behind a curtain watching the hotel fire not far away. His attention was actually directed at the female standing in the street with the white flowing hair.

"Your grandfather was a very smart man."

"Yes he was, my love. Yes he was."

Sonja closed her eyes and snuggled into his arms. This truly was her perfect day.

The next morning Sonja woke up and stretched her arms over toward where Danny was laying, only to find he was gone.

"Danny?" she called out.

The bedroom door flew open and Danny walked over with a tray of breakfast and coffee.

"I woke up early, as I usually do, and went to the market down the street to pick up a few things. You were still sleeping so I made breakfast and waited for you to wake up. Good morning, Love!" He said with a soft kiss.

She smiled and ate breakfast as they talked about the headlines in the morning paper. When she finished, Danny took the tray back to the kitchen. He returned with her coffee cup refilled.

"What are your plans for the day?" he asked.

"I think I'm hungry." She said with a slight grin as she sat up in bed.

"Didn't you just have breakfast?" he asked.

She winked at him as the covers fell off her chest. They didn't leave the apartment until noon.

Danny took Sonja to the Opera House for her afternoon practice. She had a performance that evening and had to prepare. Once she arrived, Liza, who also worked in the production behind the stage helping the girls with costumes and make-up, ran over to her and asked for all the details of the night before. The only detail that mattered was glistening on her left hand. The rest was all smiles and joy, just like the day before.

On Sonja's next day off from the ballet, they traveled back to her parents. Sonja didn't really mind going home to deliver the news. All of this news was good as far as she was concerned. Brigitte hadn't smiled so hard for so long that her face muscles were sore from it. A wedding and a grandbaby! Rudy was obviously happy. He certainly agreed that Daniel would make a fine husband. Hugo appeared pleased but continued to stay ever so stern until later that afternoon.

Hugo looked at Rudy and nodded, then left the room. Rudy leaned over to Daniel and told him to follow him. Sonja and her mother were upstairs in the house, chatting over baby names, wedding colors and things that mothers and daughters discuss about weddings and children. Sonja would remember this as one of her most fond days with her mother.

Rudy pointed to the brown door in the back of the restaurant. Danny looked at Rudy and he nodded as if to say, "Go through that door." Daniel was sure he had gained of Rudy's trust as he opened the door and followed the steps up to the second floor. The décor was very different. Polished wood that looked like mahogany. A beautiful desk and leather chairs. It wasn't a large room but very comfortable. Hugo sat in the chair behind the desk. Danny caught himself thinking, "This is what a bad guy truly thinks of himself. He thinks he's king of everything he surveys. He thinks he owns it all or deserves to own it all. This guy and what he stands for makes me sick and I'm the schmuck that saved his sorry ass. Prison won't look like this, pal."

"Take a seat, Daniel."

"I think I'll stand for a while, Hugo. It was a long ride." Danny decided not to bow to his every wish.

"I would like to discuss some business with you. Some family business. We are family now right, Daniel?"

"Of course."

"Of course we are. And family doesn't have any secrets does it, Daniel?" Hugo's question sounded more like a statement.

"Is this some kind of test? Yes, families have secrets. We all have secrets. I didn't even know my grandfather was in prison for a while. I didn't know my mother was married before she met my father. I didn't know a ton of other crap until somebody told me so. Yes, families have secrets. But it's only a secret to those who know, and the thing is knowing who's supposed to know that secret. So, if this is some kind of test, I may have just screwed it all up, but that's my opinion."

"Damn. Daniel. You pretty much just speak your mind, don't you?" Rudy said.

"Life's too short to play games, Rudy." He answered.

"He's correct." Hugo said while raising his hand so Rudy wouldn't interject anymore. And with that, Hugo began telling Daniel a bit more about the family business. He didn't exactly tell him the product right away but he did describe that the real family business was exporting. He explained about shipping, employees, hand signals, and other ways to communicate when a shipment is ready. He decided Daniel was more right than he thought. Families do have secrets and he would test Daniel with only as much of the secret as he needed to before letting him know everything. Daniel was certainly in for a test and it had only just begun.

As soon as Daniel left "The Lion's Den" as he called it, he prayed and thanked God that he had given Hugo the right answer. The weird part of all of it was that all of those secrets were really a part of his past. This may prove to work out a bit better if Hugo had any serious connections and decided to do a bit more digging into Daniel's past. Then he called Stack.

"You did what?! There's no way the section chief or the Director are going to let you complete this mission. You can't get married to the target's daughter! I won't allow it, and you don't have my blessing!" Stack was screaming into the phone so loudly that Danny was holding it away from his head.

"I thought you'd be pissed."

"Pissed! Pissed? I'm way the hell beyond pissed!" he continued to yell into the phone.

"Well, you'd better sit down. I think your blood pressure is about to go up."

"Don't tell me you botched this, Daniel. I will personally come over there and fire your ass right in front of her. If you tell me this mission is blown, you better get a job from daddy 'cuz that's the only person who will ever hire you and I will personally see to it."

"Stack!" Daniel raised his voice so Stack would listen.

"What!" Stack answered loudly since his temper was already on edge.

"LISTEN! I need you to listen to me. I really need you to hear me out. Can you just give me a minute to speak to you as my friend?" Stack's face was red with frustration – he had been pissed off at his other agents before, but this was the first time an agent took the job to a personal level. Stack didn't say a word.

"If she were a spook and I had to sleep with her to get to her boss, you wouldn't really give a crap now, would you? Don't answer that. I know you wouldn't, and I know you've probably done that yourself. It's simply the nature of our job. The mission comes first. Well the mission is still first, and no, I didn't blow it. But you need to hear all of it, Stack. It gets worse. I'm actually marrying her because I love her. I do. I know we aren't supposed to get all emotional. I get it. And I tried to ignore it, but I simply couldn't. I guess you could say I really put my heart into my work." He could feel Stack's eyes rolling up into the top of his head. "But as stupid, cliché, or corny as that sounds, it's the truth."

There was a long pause.

"Stack?"

"Daniel." Stack's tone was much lower as if he was really holding his temper. His cheeks were now turning a deep crimson color and he knew he was about to blow his top again.   Breathing slowly was all he could think about at the moment.

"Daniel. Please tell me something good because you're about to lose your job."

"No, I'm not."

"Excuse me?"

"You're not going to fire me, Stack. In fact, you're about to be very happy."

"Just how the hell do you think any of this is making me happy?"

"Well, what I've just told you about me falling in love with Sonja is true. And we are getting married. But I have more to share with you. Are you sitting down yet?"

"Oh shit. This really isn't good is it?"

"We're also going to have a baby."

"I knew it. I just knew you were headed there."

"Stack. Don't blow up. But now that you know, I want you to tell me that you're happy for us."

"Are you out of your stinking mind? I am so pissed right now. Wait, I'm beyond pissed. I'm basically numb. I'm not really sure what to say."

"I just told you what to say. Tell me you're happy for us."

"Congratulations Daniel Southerland. I'm very happy for you."

"Thank you. Now listen to this. Since the attack, which we didn't plan, and the wedding, which we didn't plan, and the baby, which we certainly didn't plan, you wouldn't have a damn thing going for us in this mission.   Which are several good reasons that you're not going to fire me. Neither you, nor I, have been able to break into this case the way we originally planned, and we haven't caught a break until now. But since all these other items have already come true, Hugo has just given me the keys to the castle."

"What do you mean 'keys to the castle'?"

"Rudy and Hugo sat down with me in his private second floor super plush gangster-style office and laid out the business. He never told me that he was trafficking girls, but he basically laid out the structure of the business, and I'm telling you, it's bigger than what either of us thought it would be. He has networked over the last twenty years and has people working for him in Oslo, Gothenburg, Stockholm, Gdansk, Amsterdam, and more. This is really huge, Stack. And if I needed a job, I've just been handed a six figure salary, which totally beats the crap out of what you guys pay me."

"Okay Daniel. You really have my attention now. What exactly do you need from me?"

"I need you to tell whoever it is you tell behind the magic curtain that I know for a fact that Sonja and Brigitte don't have a clue. Both Rudy and Hugo confirmed this. Then tell them that I'm not sorry I fell in love, just as I am equally not sorry that I will continue to complete this mission and put my future father-in-law and brother-in-law, and whomever else in the family, in prison for a very long time. Are you feeling better now, boss?"

"I'm still numb. I can't believe what I've just heard. You simply can't make this shit up! None of this was supposed to happen this way. Some white-haired girl, with a bow-and-arrow and lots of bullets, shoots up the place while you just happen to be there to save the day. All the while, you're tip-toeing in the bedroom with the ballerina and getting her pregnant, falling in love, and now marrying the daughter of the godfather of human trafficking, and you still plan on putting him behind bars. Did I get all that right?"

"That's the Reader's Digest version, but yes. Are you okay with all this now?"

"No. No I'm not at all okay with this, Daniel, but you obviously do not have a problem stepping all over the rules, guidelines, policy, and procedure. You don't care what my job description is or even if I tell you what not to do, but this is what it is and it does seem to be the only thing going for us. So tell me, Daniel, what is it you need from me now?"

"Time."

"You don't have much of that left, you know." Stack responded with a double meaning. Not much time to complete this case and probably not much time left in this job.

"I know. But since Hugo is now unknowingly giving up trade secrets to the CIA, I think it might be worth checking out if his stories are true or if he's feeding me a load of crap. I'm not too naïve to think this guy would lay a trap just to see where my loyalties lie. I've learned to listen, investigate and then educate myself on everything that is Hugo. And I wouldn't be far off base if I didn't check out a lot of his story before I throw myself on the 'smoking gun'. Hell, I pushed him away from certain death. The bullets were flying everywhere, Stack. I didn't have to knock him out of the way. I could have just let him get shot and be finished with this hell hole. But that's not the mission. Now I've just told the old guy I've been sleeping with his daughter and I'm taking her off his hands. He doesn't really care about her, but he's not the type of guy to just sit there and listen to some guy tell him what he should do with his money, especially since he's making it illegally. He needs to trust me, Stack."

"Yes, that is the mission, Danny."

"Come on, boss. You guys came up with the plan to be friends with her. Why the heck are you so pissed about my emotions?"

"Because you had them. Because we knew the weight of this mission, picked out the agent with the most talent to get the job done, and no one ever expected that you would fall in love. We made a mistake. I'm really more pissed at myself."

"No you're not. You're more pissed that when this news goes up the chain, you're going to catch hell for it. Well, it's not like I didn't try to ignore the feelings, but she's the one Stack. And I'm not sorry. I'm very happy. I'm also very happy to complete this job and put him away. I'll deal with it. The job will be done, and yes, you picked the right guy."

"We will see. So what are your plans now?"

The two of them continued their conversation and discussed how Danny should proceed.

Chapter 18

Danny prayed a lot about his next move. He is about to put away a crime boss who controlled a substantial business of human trafficking, which explained his distaste or guilt for actually having a daughter. Since Dom's death and the attack on the restaurant, Hugo rebuilt everything, fortifying the front of the building. He kept the glass windows, but he changed the design from large, single-pane sections to smaller sections with steal joints covered with stained wood. It was a very nice design and Brigitte liked it. He also built a small safe under the hostess stand and cashier desk, with a bit more ammunition and a few more Beretta M9a1's.

Hugo wasn't just busy with the restaurant front. He was also busy restructuring the roof. If he was to have a fortress, he was going to learn from the attack and do everything he could to protect himself. Hugo designed the changes himself, explaining to Brigitte that it was all for safety. Who knew when something like that could happen again? Brigitte would let him do whatever he wanted or needed for them to be safe.

Rudy was now busy doing everything with the other family business. He was in charge of more than what he was used to, and began to feel a bit overwhelmed. Hugo called him to the office and sat him down. Hugo looked at his youngest son with a bit of concern. He was still young, but Hugo remembered that he was young when he started this business. Hugo began to teach Rudy the things he had already taught Dominick. Hugo was a bit surprised to know that Rudy had already been paying attention to Dominick's work and he understood a lot of this already. (Dominick worked a larger area of the region than Rudy, and Hugo kept the two brothers more compartmentalized.) Dominick didn't know all about Rudy's territory, and it was true for Rudy as well. But now that Dom was gone, Hugo didn't trust anyone with all of this knowledge except his youngest son.

What Rudy wasn't aware of was the banking. Dominick had just begun learning that part of the business himself. Rudy was a quick study, but it was still overwhelming. One of the main differences between the brothers was that Dominick was more the strong, quiet type. He understood how to manage people and product to get results. Rudy was good at this, too, but Dominick knew how to control his emotions. As a young boy, Dom was the first to receive the backhand of Hugo's frustrations, and over time he learned to control the pain, and more importantly, how to keep his mouth shut. Rudy, on the other hand, didn't learn that lesson as quickly. Dominick may have played a role in that, too, as he tended to take the punishment from his father to save Rudy's ass. Hugo wasn't stupid, he knew what Dom was doing and allowed him to be the good older brother. However, Rudy still didn't quite learn how to keep his attitude in check all the time.

Hugo could see that this was a lot of responsibility to pile upon Rudy. Hugo didn't have to deal with an operation this huge at this age. He started off small and grew over the years. Now he was expecting Rudy to take on the leadership of several countries, a little less than a hundred employees, and all the product they transported, plus he was now learning the financial end of the business. Regardless of his age and his willingness to learn every aspect of the business, Rudy needed help.

They continued their conversation and began to slowly breach the topic of Daniel.

Daniel called Hugo, even visiting him over the next several months without Sonja. She had no desire to see her father, even though she missed her mother so much. She was doing just fine on her own, and Danny was wonderful company. She called her mother when she needed to. Her pregnancy was going well, and now she was more concerned for their child's safety. She used that and her work as excuses not to visit her hometown. She would still be able to complete all of her performances before her belly started to show a baby bump.

Weddings were supposed to take months to plan in order to be an organized day of chaos which appear as if it came off without a hitch. Those were normal weddings. Daniel agreed with Sonja that she wouldn't be getting a fairy tale wedding paid for by her father. He simply didn't care about paying for a wedding, and Brigitte probably wouldn't have a chance of persuading him. Even if she could, Sonja wasn't about to ask her. The last time the family got together for a large event, the restaurant was bullet-ridden and she nearly lost her life. Sonja and Daniel had been going to church regularly and they asked the minister if he would perform the service. Sonja asked Liza to be the maid of honor, and Daniel made this easy for everyone by asking Liza's fiancé to be the best man. The four of them calmly walked down the aisle. Sonja and Daniel walked hand-in-hand to stand at the altar. Sonja wore a white, very form-fitting above the knee pencil dress with a beautiful Bibi Satin Chapeau with a full facial veil. She was stunning and the sparkle in Daniel's eyes wasn't lost on her.

The four of them stood in the front of the church on a sunny Thursday afternoon in Oslo and the couple exchanged their vows. Sonja's tears were of joy, as were Danny's. He placed her wedding ring on her finger, raised her veil, and kissed his bride. The newlyweds left the church hand-in-hand and celebrated by having a wonderful lunch together with the wedding party. They sat outside the bistro with white wine and water, toasting to a new life together. It was a carefree atmosphere.

Daniel couldn't help but fail to notice the ice blue eyes starring across the piazza. Her white hair was covered by a black wig and her eyes were covered by oversized sunglasses as many women wore these days. She sat alone drinking an espresso, meticulously and calmly planning and doing a bit of homework on this fellow. She knew who Sonja was and what she was capable of. She was no one and capable of nothing, as far as Luna was concerned. Luna could dispatch her in a blink of an eye. However, this new husband of hers was another story. He was trained, or at least she seemed to be. If he wasn't trained, this protector was extremely brave and skilled in how to get out of an ugly situation very quickly. He did fall several times while saving Rudy. He also sprayed a lot of bullets when he killed her team. Even so, there just had to be more than just simple luck with this fellow. She found his name the week before and had begun some basic research. Her sources from Nicklaus discovered the impending wedding so she decided to come along as an uninvited guest. Upon arriving at the cathedral-style church, she decided that she shouldn't actually attend. They had no guest list, no one sitting in the pews, and no family to view the event. She couldn't quite decide if this was wise or not on their part, but she felt certain that it was planned. Was it planned to ward off unwanted visitors like herself? Was is planned to avoid another family massacre? Maybe there was some other reason she hadn't thought of, but no matter, this is certainly the way they wanted it. She thought about targeting them on their honeymoon, but she had no idea where they were going. She decided this would be the perfect time to gather her thoughts and have lunch. She didn't need any help on deciding where to go and she headed straight back to Hugo's.

Chapter 19

Rome was beautiful. They walked along the cozy, romantic streets and saw many of the touristic and historical places they both always wanted to see. Daniel didn't have an endless budget, so they chose to stay in the romantic setting of Italy. They strolled the streets and stopped by Trevi Fountain where they threw a few coins over their shoulder to signify they plan to return here again someday. They walked a short distance over to the epic Roman Coliseum. The history here was so fascinating, and the structure of the Coliseum took their breath away. They spent several hours at that location. They stopped at coffee shops, shared a few public kisses by the Pantheon, and had dinner at a small place they never expected to stop in or had even heard of before. They sat at a small, linen-covered table for two, ate their fill of a traditional Italian dinner, and toasted to the rest of their lives with a wonderful red Montepulciano d'Abruzzo. The spontaneity was wonderful. No plans but to see whatever they wanted without any timetable or schedules to keep, except to be back to complete the last few weeks of her ballet.

They spent the night in the Pantheon Hotel, a quaint hotel surrounded on three sides with narrow streets filled with people, providing room for only a single vehicle to pass through. Shops lined all three streets, and the throngs of people kept the area busy. They were lost in the tourist crowd. The front of the hotel was the Piazza della Rotonda which, of course, they could walk across to sit on the massive granite steps of the Pantheon itself. Five- to six-story hotels and apartments edged the piazza. In the center was a large stone-carved obelisk known as the Fontana de Pantheon.

Daniel awoke to their hotel room full of smoke, coughing and opening his eyes to the dark, cloudy room. He grabbed Sonja's hand and shook her awake. She stirred as he began quickly, pulling her off the bed to the floor trying to get under the smoke. Daniel's training was in high gear as he led her to the only door to the room. The door was supposed to pull open, but the knob turned without engaging. It wouldn't unlatch at all. They were choking from the smoke. He could barely see the light from their window as they crawled and coughed their way to it. Daniel tried to open it, but he couldn't open the window either. Not one to get too excited about situational complications, he simply grabbed a chair and threw it out the window. He was hoping the fire wasn't close enough to cause flash flames to engulf the room. The smoke billowed out and he could hear sirens in the distance. Knowing they didn't have much time, Daniel was actually more afraid that someone would start taking pot shots at them as they stuck their heads out the window for fresh air. Sonja's eyes were full of fear and she started remembering the attack at the restaurant. She was scared to death, screaming and crying, all the while coughing and trying to catch her breath. She was in full panic mode. Daniel sternly took Sonja's hands and looked her in the eye.

"Catch your breath, sweetheart; we will get through this. Let's start praying for help to get here quickly, and we will do whatever we need to do to get out of this building. Okay? You with me?"

Sonja nodded her head, and remembering that Daniel was quick to react. They stood next to the window and leaned over as far as they could while the black smoke billowed out. The winds were in their favor. Luna was across the Piazza del Rotunda, sitting in the third floor window just down the narrow street. Though Daniel hoped the smoke would be hiding their escape, Luna had planned for the possible weather change and already had snipers in several places in the area. People were running everywhere in the streets to help to either put out the fire or to get people out of the luxury hotel.

Daniel had already scooted back into the hotel and grabbed the sheets off the bed. Creating a slip knot he tied off one end, lifted the lion's foot bed off the floor and hooked the sheet around it. He showed Sonja the sheet and was about to direct her to climb down the sheet from their second floor room to the ground below when bullets started pinging outside the window. Daniel's fears were confirmed. He wasn't as surprised as he thought he would be. He had felt a bit uneasy the last two days, as if someone were watching him. He couldn't see which way the bullets were coming from, but he now knew they couldn't escape through the window. Sonja was even more alarmed now. She remembered the bullets from the attack at the restaurant and began screaming again. The smoke continue to get thicker and lower to the floor.

As Daniel began to retreat and regroup from the bullets at the window, the hotel room burst open. Sonya heard a muffled yell that they were here to help them but as she began to stand up to respond was overcome by the smoke and fell to her knees. Daniel thought he could nearly make out two sets of feet at the door. He was about to make his way toward the firemen when he heard the distinct sound of suppressed gun shots. Sonja could also hear it and she squeezed his hand even tighter. Daniel pulled her close to him and then carefully pushed her just behind the end of the large dresser that was at the end of the bed. He was changing her position in the room and protecting her as much as he could. He then kissed her hand and let it go. He stood and grabbed the lamp from on top the dresser and threw it against the opposite wall causing a distraction. As soon as the lamp crashed against the wall, Daniel could see the muzzle flash. He did a shoulder roll, inhaled while he was closest to the floor and came up right beside the shooter. Grabbing the pistol, he noticed the second shooter, and jumping high in the air, he threw his body into him, legs first, hitting him in the chest. He held onto the pistol and pulled it over the man's shoulder. The gun fired again into the ceiling. Sonja was freaking out in the corner. She was as low to the floor as she could be and could barely make out three sets of feet.

Daniel twisted his attacker's arm and made him fire his own weapon into his own brain. Grabbing the gun, he quickly shot in the direction of the other man and heard the bullet hit his target. As soon as he landed on the floor, Daniel shot him again.

Daniel checked the hallway and it was clear. He quickly ran back for Sonja who needed oxygen very badly. He led her out of the room and down the stairs. Knowing bullets would come at them from the front of the building, he was sure the back would be watched, too, so the basement was the best option. This was the reason he chose this hotel. He knew the old architecture still had hidden passages underneath, and while the building was built so long ago, it wasn't so long ago that they were used. He had done this before during an extraction several years ago.

Luna searched through the crowd of running people scurrying the piazza. She called her team over the radios, but no one spotted them. She had failed again. She hated failure. Sonja had to die! She was blood kin from the man who had ruined her life and she was going to make Hugo pay. She was going to make him wish he had never started exporting women and young girls. Luna was going to remove all of his family legacies and then she would watch him beg for his life.

Chapter 20

The day before the wedding, Luna sat in her hotel room, paid for by Nicklaus, and looked at herself in the mirror. She was strikingly beautiful. Ice blue eyes, brilliant white hair, toned body from working out daily and voluptuous, in a very athletic way. She was a head turner in a man's world, and for some women as well. Today she would have to tone down her looks. Today was a research day, not a day of killing. Today would be full of focus, control and denying one's self of pure gratification.

She put on her dark black wig and brown contact lenses. She used makeup, but her features still made her attractive. She wore a very modest top and slightly baggy pants. She picked out an old pocketbook that was worn with age, putting in just enough money to cover lunch and cab fare.

She grabbed a cab and told the driver to head to Hugo's. After a short drive across town, she found herself sitting in the restaurant where she so recently helped to kill several people.

Her gut was spitting out nails at the hatred she was feeling, but her voice was quite elegant as she spoke to Brigitte.

"Good afternoon. What would you like to have for lunch today?" Brigitte asked politely. Luna ordered lunch and began a little small talk with Brigitte. Polite and kind, Luna complimented Brigitte on the wonderful decor of the restaurant. However, she said, "I thought I remembered pictures of your children on the walls. No?"

"Yes, it's true. We used to have pictures on the walls, but recent remodeling didn't allow sufficient space for all the pictures I would like to hang." Brigitte was talking like a mother, and that's exactly where Luna wanted her to go.

"What family pictures would you hang?" Luna asked.

Slight tears welled up on Brigitte's eyes. "I would hang a picture of my Dominick. He was my oldest. He died in a car wreck not too long ago."

"Oh! I'm so sorry to hear that."

"Then there's my Rudy. My only boy now."

Luna's mouth began to water as she thought of the way she would be killing Rudy. "Are those all your children?"

"No. I also have a daughter who she has found a very nice young man to marry. I would like to put a picture of their wedding on the wall someday."

"Oh, how I love wedding pictures. When did they marry?" Luna began her research with this question.

"Just a moment dear, let me go seat the people at the door. I shall be right back," and Brigitte excused herself.

Luna's internal thermostat rose a bit due to the delay, but she remembered to stay focused, nodding her head as Brigitte walked away.

Brigitte returned with Luna's order and fell right back into the conversation. She's getting married in Oslo in a couple days. Oh, how I wish I could be there."

"You're not going?"

"We cannot go. We've already had to close down for the funeral and all the remodeling. There's only so much we can do." Brigitte said sullenly.

"And where do they plan to honeymoon? It must be somewhere very romantic." Luna said with a smile and wishful face as if she had been dreaming of a romantic honeymoon of her own.

"They are headed to Rome. She just called me this morning and told me the news. Come to think of it, you're the first person I've told." Brigitte touched her shoulder as if they had been friends for a long time. Luna smiled back as warmly as she could while realizing her plan was working just as she wanted. She continued to make small talk, finished her lunch, waived to Brigitte and left the restaurant. After catching a cab back to her hotel, she began making calls to three of her best men.

Luna was able to find out what hotel 'Mr. and Mrs. Southerland' were staying in based on the conversation with Brigitte. She also found out what church in Oslo they would be married in. Luna was having to decide exactly where she was going to kill them. Sonja was a must, and this new man was a bonus.

There would probably be many family members at the wedding, she thought. But then again, this wedding was a fairly sudden event as far as she could tell from the conversation with Sonja's mother. Luna was quite happy that Brigitte was so forthcoming with information, not knowing it would be the end of her daughter's life. Killing Brigitte later could be bitter sweet.

After several hours of personal deliberation, Luna came to the conclusion that the honeymoon would be the better option. If they were spooked by having a large family gathering, then the intimate setting could be less of a place to be on their guard.

Luna placed two men in the hotel on the same floor as the honeymoon suite. She picked these two men for their paramilitary training in close-quarter combat. She gave them MP5s and two extra clips, allowing for ninety rounds per man. She also told each man to carry any other compact weapons they felt they may need for a job such as this. She wanted them to feel confident they could complete the task. For her part, she would be waiting across the piazza where she could see the entire front of the hotel just in case they tried to escape by their only window. She had already walked through the hotel and found the honeymoon suite's view of the landing below their window. The third man was placed down the side street in case they ran out the side entrance along with the other people staying there. Exits were covered. Plenty of ammunition. The plan was in place.

Luna decided to confuse the couple by starting a fire. Her plan was to catch them off guard in their sleep, enter the room clothed as firefighters, shoot them both and leave their bodies to burn without much evidence of gun play. If necessary, she was mentally prepared to allow for several innocent people to die to cover up her mess, but that was within tolerable limits to her. She didn't care about them at all. Even if the entire guest list of the hotel were shredded by bullets, she was apathetic. Luna wanted Sonja dead ~ today. Luna and her third man shouldn't have to worry about a thing if all went well and her plan rarely fail.

A fire started on the floor just below the Southerland's. The flames expanded to each room quickly due to the accelerant. As the smoke began to escape the building, people started running around the piazza, and real firefighters would be on their way soon. She peered through the scope when she saw it. A sheet thrown through the window. She waited until she could see a body. She knew it would be Sonja, as men always save the women or children first. However, Luna didn't want them to die by gunfire in public, so she sent a few rounds to the window. The window ledge burst apart, and she saw Southerland's hand grab Sonja, pulling her back into the room and certain death.

Feeling certain they would not try the window again, she quickly packed her weapon and moved to a new vantage point where she had a closer view. Real firefighters were now onsite, bringing people out. No one resembled Sonja or her new husband was in the crowd. Luna smiled a bit as she was thinking how this plan was working. She radioed the sniper down the block who replied he hadn't seen the targets leave the building.

She radioed her two attackers inside the building, but when she didn't receive an answer, she began to get frustrated. She couldn't go into the burning building. The authorities wouldn't allow it. The flames were at their worst now so all she could do was wait. She was beginning to pace a bit in the street, her white hair blowing in the breeze, watching the flames engulf the building. If her men didn't

Chapter 21

Sonja sat on the edge of the bed, so very confused. Why was all this happening to them? First her father's restaurant, and now their honeymoon. "What the hell is going on, Daniel? I'm a simple ballerina and you're a financial analyst who fell in love with me. I bring you to my family's restaurant, and somebody tries to rob and kill us, but you saved our lives. We get married and someone tries to burn our hotel, shoot at us, and you save us again! What the hell did I do to deserve someone trying to kill me?"

Daniel had been thinking about this moment for a while. He already infuriated his boss by telling him the truth, stepping outside the policies and falling in love with an innocent party but still within the parameters of his case. On top of that, he married her! He couldn't avoid the conversation that was about to follow. He had to tell her everything. He wanted no secrets between the two of them as enemies could use this against them if provided the opportunity.

"Sonja, my love, we need to have a chat about all this, shall we?" he asked.

"Oh my! Daniel I am so very sorry you had to go through all this. I promise I don't know why this is happening!" she began to sob.

"I'm not sorry, Sonja. I've been there twice now when you needed me, and I want to be there every time you need me. I absolutely love you."

"And I you," she said with a smile, wiping the tears from her face.

"I'm going to tell you a story, Sonja. Before you begin to ask questions, please hear the words I tell you. Okay?" Sonja looked a bit puzzled, but nodded her head yes.

Daniel began with his childhood, including a few stories she hadn't already heard. He then told her stories of a horrible man who had been ruining countless young girl's lives by drugging them, kidnapping them and shipping them to other parts of the world - explaining that this man was the biggest human trafficker in his region, and that neither his wife nor his daughter knew about it.

Sonja was slowly getting the picture, but kept her emotions in check. She was beginning to shed tears again, but this time was more from shock. Daniel continued to explain to her how this made him feel and she wholeheartedly agreed with him. Then he began to tell her how he had always wanted to help people and to put away those who hurt others. Sonja could see the Boy Scout in him, again confirming in her mind that he was wonderful man.

Up to this point, he was pretty much in a safe zone, but that was about to change.

"Sonja, your father asked me if we were family. I said yes. He also asked me if families kept secrets. Again, I said yes, and told him about some of my own family secrets which I learned long after those secrets were old news, but it was new to me. Do you understand this?"

"Yes, I think I do." she said wondering where this conversation was going.

This is where the sting is about to happen. He slowly unraveled the mystery of his job, something he wasn't ever supposed to do. At this point he explained that was the reason he was able to save her during both of these attacks. She sort of smiled at actually having her very own bodyguard and that he actually loved her. This part went a whole lot better than expected. He questioned her about his cover job, just to be sure she understood what he actually did for a living. She nodded, looked at him with her innocent eyes and said, "You save the world and most recently you saved me. I think I'm okay with this."

"Sonja. Do you remember how we met?"

"Of course I do silly. It's not been that long ago."

"That has been and will always be one of my very best memories. I never knew I would fall in love that night, and I'm so very glad I did. My love for you is very real. And I want it to last forever."

"As do I, Daniel."

"Why, thank you, Mrs. Southerland," he replied with a genuine smile and continued.

"Sonja, the part of my job that makes this so different than others isn't necessarily the secret parts. It's knowing who all the players are, knowing the secrets they know, and knowing when to tell those secrets to someone who really should know them. Does that make sense?" He waited for her reaction.

"Isn't that a bit childish? Just tell the truth!" She made it sound so simple.

"I wish the world was that simple, my love, but it is not. And now comes the part where I tell you something that you need to know. I do not know the person who is after us. I've only seen her once before today, and that was at your father's restaurant. She was the one, I believe, who tried to kill your father." He paused and she said nothing. "I saw her again today. She was down on the piazza by our hotel. She may still be lurking around, but I'm quite sure we're safe right here." He could see her shoulders tensing up, fear creeping into her expressions. Daniel wasn't afraid of awkward silences. This is when questions were asked internally, and on occasion, people figured out their own answers.

"Daniel, why do you think she was trying to kill my father and she is here trying to kill us? Could this be another case, a case that's more about you?"

"Great question. But I have no idea who she is, and I have only had one case to concentrate on in the three months before I meeting you." He waited for the inevitable question.

"Are you allowed to tell me the case?"

"No. But I'm going to anyway. I'm investigating the man I told you about earlier. The man who steals young girls away, drugs them, gets them hooked on drugs and then sells them as slaves to the highest bidder miles away from their homes and who has done so for a very long time."

"Do you think she was one of those girls, this girl you saw today?"

"I do."

"Then why do you think she would try to kill my...." Sonja didn't finish her sentence. She had suddenly picked up on everything Danny had said. Her face flushed with a horrible resentment. She stood up and ran to the bathroom and vomited. Danny followed, but kept his distance. He knew Sonja well enough that she would come to him when she accepted the knowledge that her father was more of a monster than she had ever known him to be.

Danny rinsed a small cloth with cool water and handed it to Sonja as she sat in the bathroom floor. Her face was flushed and her eyes were red. She slowly looked up at him. "But I truly love you, Danny. I am not a toy in this game of secrets am I?"

"I absolutely love you. I've never been so in love in my entire life, and I never want secrets to come between us. This is why you had to know. You *needed* to know Sonja. I need you to understand my love is all yours, but my job is saving people. Right now my job is putting your father in prison."

"And yet you saved his life at the restaurant."

"I don't want him dead. He is still your father. And my boss needs to know about the entire operation to shut it down. Plus, there were a lot of other innocent people there, including your mother. I don't believe she has ever known about his business. He has truly mastered the art of deception."

"She must be very angry, this girl with the white hair. Why do you think she is trying to kill me?"

"Most likely because you and your mother are the only two women we know whom he has never harmed. I think she plans to take that away from him as he took her normal life away from her. It's the only thing that makes sense."

He had no idea how right he was. He was also so very grateful he spent time with Sonja and told her everything. He was a very lucky man to have found this beautiful and understanding lady. This conversation could have really gone the other way and been so much worse. He could only hope that this wouldn't cause problems for them in the future.

Sonja looked up at Danny with worry in her face. "My mother! You have to save my mother!"

Chapter 22

Rudy's new position in the family business afforded him new opportunities than he had before. His big brother wasn't there looking over his shoulder anymore. His father didn't venture out of the restaurant as he used to do, either. Since a few key family members were also killed in the attack by the White Witch, things were a bit dicier. Adding to this was Nicklaus's plan to fan the flames of the power and fear of the White Witch. He led everyone to believe he controlled her. Not to mention the scary name he called her portrayed an untouchable image. There was definitely more stress on Rudy than Dominick had ever felt. His father was having a harder time getting people to work for him. The loyalty factor was certainly the biggest issue. The reputation of the White Witch was new, but fighting for loyal employees wasn't a problem until now. The downside for Rudy was his maturity and his leadership style.

Dom had seen the way his father treated his employees. Hugo was not a man of compromise. Over time, his reputation was proven. If you did the job exactly as you were instructed, you would never be fired. Should you not perform to his satisfaction, you were taught a lesson by way of humiliation and pain. While the pain was intense, the humiliation was something so much harder to overcome. Only a few of Hugo's employees ever tested his methods, and only two of them lived to learn their lesson. The others weren't fired from the job; they were eliminated after the pain and humiliation. Hugo made the humiliation more public when he planned to remove the employee from his payroll. Hugo allowed the other neighborhood gangs to hear about his noncompliance benefits. In one instance, he allowed others to see the human degradation he put his low-performing, disobedient employee through in order to prove the rumors as true. This instilled more fear and respect for his business. If he would treat his own employees in such a manner, what more would he be willing to do if he was your enemy?

Now that the rivals had this White Witch character, Hugo's intimidation factor was slowly diminishing. No one had ever even dared to try to put Hugo's business at risk. No one had ever thought of taking any of it away from him. His network didn't have any borders and it didn't really interfere with other gangs' profits, except for a few of the prostitutes who disappeared, and in those cases, no one could ever prove it was Hugo's doing.

Hugo was still in unquestionable command, but his network knew that Dominick was on the rise to step into the position whenever Hugo made that decision. However, there were hesitations with the thought of Rudy stepping up. He had recently been given his territory and he was still learning. He was quite respected in the organization as the son of Hugo. The people he already commanded were comfortable with him. Now, his quiet nature was something he would need to overcome to show that he can command the entire corporation. Dom's team was accustomed to his own style of leadership. A totally different personality than that of Hugo. Rudy didn't raise his voice much. He knew he had much to learn and much more to prove. He also had one weakness. He had been concealing it from Hugo for as long as he could remember - his little sister.

Chapter 23

Months later, everything seemed to have gotten back to normal. Hugo slowly restructured the business, and as expected, Rudy was elevated to control the family business. Rudy's personality was actually more widely accepted than anticipated. His quiet nature was more ominous than Dom's loud vocal displays. Rudy commanded more fear than Hugo expected, and he was pleasantly surprised. One of Rudy's first decisions was met with some resistance from one of Dom's men. Within a two-hour window, Rudy found out for himself if he had the guts to make the tough decisions. Hugo heard of the swift decision process and he approved. The employee was found in a local bar and was escorted to a waterfront warehouse where his loyalty to Hugo and Rudy was tested. Some of the painful parts of this discipline would eventually heal, but not all. This was Rudy's first major disciplinary action and he had to make a statement. They weren't sure if this associate could stand the humiliation. He was castrated in front of his wife and several other associates who might need some visual understanding of what it means not to be loyal to Hugo.

Brigitte ran the restaurant's daily activities, still not knowing what Hugo had been hiding from her for so long. She handled the restaurant employees like family. She wasn't always a happy lady, but always polite to customers, and the food was always made to perfection. The sales were slow after the incident but had slowly returned to normal.

Daniel steadily gained Hugo's trust even without Rudy's and Brigitte's urging. Being married to his daughter had no part in Hugo's decision to trust Danny. The fact that he fought courageously and without reservation against an unknown opponent gave Hugo something to consider. That and he really understood financial growth in a manner that wouldn't send him to prison, so he allowed him a bit of knowledge into the finances of the export business. Hugo reinforced the roof security area with a few more iron shields for protection from other buildings. He reloaded the weapons box and added a few more locks. Daniel told him about the White Witch being on the roof and now, to Hugo's knowledge, only he, Daniel, Rudy and that nasty witch knew of those weapons. Hugo had to trust Daniel with this information as well. Daniel was fairly honest when he told Hugo that he wanted no part of any combinations, keys, or information how to access the secure four lockboxes. What he didn't say was that he was able to find out what system Hugo bought to secure those weapons and already knew how to get into them.

Hugo still wouldn't tell him the products or shipping details, and Daniel's handler was about to pull the plug on this whole operation. Stack's superiors were furious at Daniel, trying to get him pulled off the case and fired, but someone from higher up in the CIA saw this as the biggest opportunity they had against Hugo. Daniel was the first man to ever come from outside the family to be a part of the organization. So what if he fell in love along the way. Many of the operatives had feelings, and Daniel Southerland simply acted on it. It was clearly against policy, and he will be dealt with once this operation was over, but until then, the agency decided to leave him alone. Stack didn't know who was protecting Daniel and he didn't care. He agreed.

Luna had been planning a nice little party for Hugo. She was a few weeks away from springing the surprise. She had a few more details to accomplish before she could press the go button, staying out of site and away from Nicklaus. She didn't want to draw attention to herself. The rumors that she was still in town kept Nicklaus' associates at a heightened level of caution. Nicklaus would threaten to call her if any of his men got out of line. She did, however, take a monthly trip to the restaurant wearing a black wig and makeup. Her first visit with Brigitte was quite revealing, and she hoped the informative relationship might flourish. The hardest part was hiding her hatred for Hugo.

Chapter 24

Sonja's show had run its course, and a new ballet had already begun. She had several months of fabulous reviews. She clipped all of the newspaper articles, adding them to her scrapbook. She also continued her studies at the university, but her mind was more concentrated on her pregnancy. She was now thirty-seven weeks and was feeling ready for this to be over. "Danny!" she said very loudly.

He jumped off the edge of the couch and landed on his heels, nearly falling over. He had been napping after lunch and her yelling caused him to reach for his sidearm. She smiled from across their apartment from where she was sitting on the edge of their bed. He may be a trained professional, but that was quite funny. She was actually glad she found humor despite the fact she was ready to head to the hospital. She always heard women were really panicky at this point in the pregnancy, however, she was surprisingly calm. She placed her right hand under her stomach and steadily stood up. She walked into the living room, picked up her purse and looked in his direction.

"Grab the hospital go bag, sweetheart. It's baby time," she announced. Danny gathered himself, grabbed her pre-packed hospital bag, took hold of Sonja's hand and walked her to the car. Sonja had tried several times recently to ride in the front seat, but she just couldn't seem to fit in comfortably. Danny opened the back passenger door and helped her get in. She was most comfortable with several pillows, placing her legs on the bench seat of their white Mercedes 300d that Danny found for a bargain price. He chose this as it would carry Sonja and their kids with enough room for luggage for their future vacations. She actually hated it. The previous owner had cut a hole in the top of the car and covered it with leather. Someone ruined a perfectly beautiful piece of machinery so they could act like fools and stick their heads out or wave their arms in the air. Why the hell didn't they just buy a convertible? She really didn't like it at all. Daniel had always wanted a rag top. He loved convertibles but thought better of it with a child on the way. He checked out the construction of this leather sun roof and it was of professional quality. It wasn't just cut open in someone's garage with a chainsaw. The edges were cut and rounded, and weather stripping sealed the seams. The salesman swore it was weatherproof. Plus, he had other things to consider. When carrying a child, would the car be too cold in the winter? If the top were pushed open, would it be too windy in the summer? There was so much to think about when taking a newborn into consideration, and even then, as the child got older but not yet thinking logically, would the child try to climb out while the car was in motion?

Well, this car had it all, and he believed it was a great compromise. Sonja still wasn't a fan, but after he explained all of his reasons, she found him so thoughtful that it simply wasn't worth arguing over. Besides, she hadn't ever actually owned a car. She had always relied on her brothers or public transportation. She thought about this for a moment when she first saw the car. This was her first of many things. Her first love, her first child, her first car - her world was totally new since she met Daniel, and he kept surprising her all the time. She smiled at Daniel as she was finally sitting so the baby wasn't pressing against her lungs. "I'm ready to do this. The baby is ready, too," she said in an excitedly painful voice as the baby kicked.

They drove north from their apartment. They passed the Royal Place where they enjoyed several of their summer dates sitting in the grass enjoying the sun. The Oslo Rikshospitalet was located by the university, north of the main part of town. They didn't have much knowledge about the medical system in Norway so they each did a little homework in the last few months. Sonja had heard that most everyone used a midwife who would stay with you from when you hired her all the way through the birthing process. Danny was more accustomed to having an actual doctor take care of all things medical as was traditional in the United States. Neither of them was going to argue the points too much so they compromised on both. Daniel found a doctor who would see them. He used the excuse that the attack at the hotel could have caused some complications with the baby, and Sonja readily agreed to see him once a month for checkups. Sonja wasn't aware, but this particular doctor was recommended by several of the local CIA operatives whom Daniel trusts. For reasons no one would come right out and say, those operatives were rather adamant that he use Dr. Kreagor. Sonja found a midwife who answered all her questions whenever she needed to call. She also helped them by explaining the birthing process and what to expect so that neither of them would have any surprises.

During one of the doctor's visits a few months back, Dr. Kreagor asked them both to come into the examination room. Sonja walked over to the long table with the white sheet hanging over it and sat down. Danny took a seat in the straight-backed chair just to the left.

"Today is the day we should do a sonogram. Do you know what that is?" Dr. Kreagor asked.

"When you take a picture of the baby?" Sonja answered a bit excited, glancing at Danny for his reaction. On cue, Danny was smiling.

"Yes, basically. I do not always perform a sonogram, but in your case I have some questions and this is the best way to determine if I am right."

"What exactly are you trying to determine, and what do you think is wrong? Is the baby okay?" Sonja's asked worriedly as Daniel stood up.

"Ok. Have a seat Daniel. And yes, Mrs. Southerland, everything is fine. Please, this is just a precaution. I am not worried about anything. I simply need some clarification to prepare for the delivery." Dr. Kreagor was quite nice and very sure that everything would be fine. "Come with me Mrs. Southerland." The doctor helped her off the table and down the hall into another room with a large machine. The nurse helped her lie down on the table. The nurse raised her shirt to uncover her belly, and applied some sort of gel to allow for a clearer picture of the child.

The doctor was standing to one side beside a large cabinet-style machine with a monitor screen. There were a lot of buttons and dials on the machine. The nurse reached across Sonja's abdomen, grabbing a large camera-looking device on a long mechanical arm. The mechanical arm was attached to a large brick-like device with a smooth rounded surface on one side. The nurse slowly smoothed gel over Sonja's belly, and images began to appear on the monitor. Sounds could be heard as the doctor would tell the nurse where to guide the ultrasound hand piece.

The doctor spent several minutes without speaking, when finally he said, "Okay, parents. Just as I suspected, everything is quite fine. No problems at all. And I do believe that the both of you will make very fine parents, too. I do." And he smiled very big.

"So everything is really ok? Healthy? Nothing to worry about?" Sonja was looking for reassurance. Danny held her hand a bit tighter and said, "He just confirmed all is going to be fine." The doctor nodded his head in approval. "Would you like to know the gender?"

Sonja looked at Danny and he looked at the doctor and said, "We've discussed this recently and she left that up to me. I'm sort of an old-fashioned guy and I enjoy the suspense. God has blessed us in so much lately, and I think we shouldn't ruin his surprise for us. Don't tell us. We will learn soon enough."

"Ahhhhh! You are among the few people after my own heart! Very well then. A surprise it shall be!" The nurse helped Sonja take care of herself, and the two of them left the hospital with a few more instructions about eating enough, not lifting too much and last-minute details.

They were still several miles away from Rikshospitalet when a small, black sedan wouldn't leave Daniel's rearview mirror. He decided to make a few direction changes just to be sure. As soon as he made a second right-hand turn, changing directions away from Oslo Hospital, Sonja looked at him in the rearview mirror and was about to say something when she saw the look in his eyes.

"Buckle up, sweetheart. Let's make this a safe ride." He looked directly back at her with hopes that this wasn't what he thought it was.

Chapter 25

Luna was glad she had been eating at the restaurant every now and then. While masking her hatred and planning Hugo's demise, she was actually enjoying the food. There was something about being so close to this man she hated and who had no idea that his death was imminent. She could think of fifty different ways to kill him every time he walked past her table. Once he was killed, she would take out everyone else in the building and casually walk away before the cops showed up. She looked around the room and noticed that everything had a weapon. Certainly she carried her own weapons with her, but the everyday tools that many people didn't consider as a tool that was capable of killing them was sitting on the table. The cloth napkins, the pretty table cloths, pens, silverware, Brigitte's apron, the glassware, chairs, tables and anything else she could see were all tools that she could use to remove a threat. She felt very powerful during those moments. She also felt her blood pressure rise when Hugo stood near the front door glaring at the family's young girls who walked in. She wondered just how many families Hugo had ruined. Did he think about taking those two young girls who just walked in without their parents? Or did he just prey on the kids who were lost and on the streets without any family to come looking for them? Either way, she was infuriated every time he walked by to cheerfully greet another family into his humble food establishment.

"Brigitte?" she asked. "How are things with you lately? I'm afraid I haven't been able to stop by as often as I would have liked. How is everyone? Please, help me catch up with the news of your family." Luna sat in the booth on the right side of the restaurant wearing a white satin button up blouse with a lace camisole, black slacks a business jacket and matching black heels. She looked as if she just walked out of a board meeting, and acted as if she barely had time to eat.

"Hello, my friend. I could use a bit of a break about now so I'm going to go get two glasses of wine and we can visit for a bit."

Moments later she returns with two glasses of red table wine, holding the bottle under one arm. She set the glasses and the bottle on the table, picked up her own glass and they touched their glasses as if they were going to toast a special occasion. Without saying a word, they both lifted their glasses of wine ever so slightly, each taking a healthy sip.

"I tell you, things have been slowly coming back to life around here. Hugo and I are pretty much doing everything ourselves. All of our children have gone away from us and we only have a handful of employees. They all work very hard, but some days I truly wish my children were near me again."

"I did notice your youngest boy was not around." Luna pushed for an answer.

"Yes. My boy, Rüdiger, is a very busy man. He has taken a job that makes him travel and that keeps him away from the restaurant. He was very good at keeping all of our supplies here stocked. I had to learn what he did and every delivery schedule. We used to have two local boys who worked at the market deliver to us, but now we can't seem to get the same boy two weeks in a row. I do not know what Rudy did to make it happen, but it's not quite the same. They can't seem to deliver at the same time and I don't always get everything I ordered." Brigitte stopped and took another sip of wine.

"What about other family members helping you out, Brigitte? Can't some other family come to help?" Luna was leading her right down the path.

"Several of the family members did come for a while after the attack, but they already had a life before that day and couldn't stay. Oh, and I miss my Dominick so much."

"I'm so sorry, Brigitte. I shouldn't have asked." Luna put on a sad face.

"No, my dear. There is nothing you can do and yours is a valid question. One that is still met with sadness on my part, but don't you worry about it. I am a strong woman." Brigitte patted Luna's hand several times.

"But today I do have some good news! My daughter, Sonja, will be going to the hospital tomorrow to have her baby!" Brigitte said with a huge smile.

Luna's face went blank for a moment. She could tell her temperature was rising. She was about to be very angry when she notice Brigitte holding up her glass as if to do another toast. Luna shook off her red face and lifted her glass.

"How wonderful," she said as she quickly recovered. And the first obvious question spewed out of her mouth.

"What hospital will she be going to?"

"Oh! She is in Oslo with her husband. He just left from here last week. As with most men, he didn't know when the baby would arrive. Sonja just called me a little bit ago and said she would be going to the hospital tomorrow. She does not know if it will be a boy or a girl, but I am hoping for a girl! We have so many boys in this family and I think I need a little pink coloring in my life. But for some reason I think it will be a boy. She just carries that child like it's a boy," Brigitte said with bright eyes.

"A little boy." Luna again could feel her blood begin to boil. Hugo would get a new heir to the family's "other business" and train him to be as hateful as all the other men of Hugo's family. This was something she simply could not allow.

Chapter 26

Luna and Brigitte finished their conversation and the rest of the bottle of wine. Luna excused herself for the evening. She paid for her meal, saying goodbye to Brigitte, maybe for the last time. Luna's mind was racing to plan her next move. She had to find just the right men to do the job without screwing it up this time. She would not underestimate this man. A man with skills like his was uncommon. Even in her own profession, he would be considered exceptional. She tried to find out any background information on him and little came up except routine tidbits. He kept to himself even though he had remarkable skills. He was always under the radar while performing in the top five percent of everyone at his job. She didn't think he had any clue to what Hugo's true business was, but that didn't matter to her. His new wife was the target and he was in the way. Poor fellow didn't know what was coming.

Luna caught the next plane to Oslo. She already had a bag packed with her personal gear that would pass through the airport. When she landed, she found her driver waiting for her with the back door open. On the seat next to her was a shiny black briefcase. The driver shut her door, got back in the car and she barked directions and more orders for her plan. Luna opened the case to find a Ruger .22 caliber MK II. The barrel was threaded and the silencer was seated in its place just above the weapon. This particular professional target weapon was considered accurate up to 70 meters, but Luna was sure she would be much closer.

Luna reached for her own luggage on the floorboard, unzipping it. She pulled out a full black form-fitting pant suit. She stripped off her red blouse, black skirt and heels. Sitting in the back seat in nothing but her black lace panties, she noticed the driver's head wasn't checking the traffic any longer. The driver was wearing sunglasses but his head was fixed on the mirror. "Drive," she said calmly as she watched his head refocus. He knew better than to speak. As soon as she was dressed, she pulled off her red wig, revealing her pure white hair as she put on her dark sunglasses.

They stopped at Hemingbanen, a local sports complex with a Tramway stop, just north of the hospital where Brigitte thought they would be going. She assigned her three-man team to separate locations around the area to spot the couple. All three cars were to look exactly alike, and each man was to be dressed in a black suit, white shirt and black tie. No exceptions. They would also carry the exact same weapon she carried. She passed out radios and earwigs. They looked more like CIA operatives than private mercenaries, which is exactly what she wanted. As soon as this mission was over, they would all be paid very handsomely.

"The target is the female. The trouble is the male. When you get to her, kill her. I do not care that she is carrying a child. You all understand this, yes? I do not care if you leave the man alive or not, but he will be your biggest problem. Do not underestimate him. He is very resourceful. He is her only protection, and this is going to end today. Do you understand?" Luna was very blunt as she waited for each man to confirm that she would not stand for any failure.

As the three black sedans left the parking lot to cover the main routes into the hospital, Luna took the Tramway heading north. She knew exactly where her targets would end up even before they did.

About an hour later, the first black sedan spotted the white Mercedes and turned around to follow. He radioed his location so all four of them knew exactly where he was. In a few short minutes he was about 100 yards behind them when the Mercedes turned right. He had very precise instructions not to lose them. However, he soon felt a gut feeling that he had been spotted. The Mercedes took another right turn and he had no choice but to continue with the pursuit. The other sedans hadn't caught up to him yet. They were supposed to corral Mr. Southerland, lead him away from the hospital, and directly toward the lady with the white hair.

Without thinking, the driver pulled out his silenced .22 and began to fire. The bullets plinked off the side of the car, increasing the driver's fear. His reaction caused the Mercedes to change directions again.

The second thug had been listening to the first driver about every directional change. He was just a few minutes away when he heard the message that the first car had been seen. The Mercedes was now heading right for him.

The very narrow streets of Oslo were much like driving through a small hallway. But now it felt even smaller when the first driver started shooting. The .22 caliber bullets weren't fatal at this point since the Mercedes was manufactured with such heavy gauge metal, causing the rounds to bounce off. They did, however, produce the desired effect and the Mercedes drove faster. Luna's driver wouldn't mind if the Mercedes had a terrible wreck, killing both occupants. Likewise, Luna didn't care if they died a scary and painfully bloody death in a car wreck or by the quick, efficient bullets placed directly in their skull. Dead is dead and that's exactly what she wanted. Luna wasn't prideful on this particular kill. Sonja's husband was certainly making this more interesting, but she wasn't going to lose this battle today.

Chapter 27

Luna was listening to the radio traffic as she sat on the tram. Since her first attack on the restaurant, she had been doing a lot of homework on all of Hugo's family which now, unfortunately, included Daniel Southerland. She was able to use Nicklaus's contacts within the local police, but those contacts didn't produce any noteworthy results. Thinking proactively, she broadened her research to include a member of the Norwegian State Police, smiling as she remembered meeting the Police Inspector.

Jørgen Solberg wasn't a rising star in the NSP, but he worked hard to reach the rank of Police Inspector. Luna had spent the last six weeks slowly following him and making mental notes of all of his daily habits. She watched him sit in a small café nearly every morning for the first week. He would sit at his regular table right inside the café, drink his coffee as he read the morning edition of the local paper, *Aftenposten*. The paper had a daily readership of just over 200,000. She watched from several different angles, disguising herself every time. She noticed he would read for about thirty seconds, then shift his eyes above the top of the paper and look around. He was either nervous or suspicious, and she wasn't sure which. Once he finished his coffee, he would work until 5:30 and return to the same café. He was certainly a creature of habit. It was evident the café was where he felt most comfortable. This is where she would insert herself into his life.

Luna wondered how to get this odd character of a man to tell her what she wanted to know -how she would get him to tell her things without giving up her plan. She decided to work him the same way she worked Brigitte, but with a little twist.

She wasn't sure how much time she would have to gather information about Mr. Southerland or if she could even get her target to talk, but this was her best option given all the other scenarios she had come up with. She sat down right outside the café at the table by the window. He would have no choice but to see her every time he looked out the window. She dressed in casual clothes at first, wearing her auburn wig which fit perfectly, allowing her to pull it back into a ponytail. This made her neck look longer and the opening of her button up shirt look deeper. She ordered the same coffee as he did, placing her notebook and maps on the table, giving the appearance she was working on some sort of research. She had several books about the architecture of the surrounding buildings. She would point to several articles in the book and then use a camera and take pictures of the building and create some corresponding notes. She repeated this routine for several days, finally deciding to get to the café just a few minutes before he did and make herself known.

She stood in line and ordered her coffee. She spoke English to appear as a tourist. He was third in line. She paid for her coffee and sat in "his" chair and "his" table. He noticed immediately that this pretty young lady was in his spot. This didn't sit well with him and she could see him becoming a bit fidgety. So she crossed her legs, showing a bit more of her thigh. She pretended to read the paper and could hear his footsteps coming directly toward her.

In his native language he spoke politely to her. "Good morgon, Fru. Godt å sjå deg!" He was trying to tell her 'Good Morning. It's nice to meet you.'" But as soon as he completed his sentence, she looked up very confused and embarrassed.

"I'm so sorry. I'm not from here. I'm American." She made her cheeks turn just a bit pinker than normal so her embarrassment would seem real.

"Ah! Well I speak English as well. My name is Inspector Solberg."

"Wonderful! I love meeting new people. Please, would you join me?" Her invitation didn't give him time to tell her to leave "his" table as she moved her leg under the table and pushed the chair across from her.

"Tell me, Inspector, how much history do you know about Oslo? I have to write a historical piece, and I would love to pick your brain about some of these wonderful places you have in your city. These books have a lot of dry information with no real stories to make me feel as if I can write anything that hasn't already been written. I'm rather lost at the moment." She looked at him with the same emotion she just spewed out at him.

"Well, Miss?" He politely waited for her name.

"Miss Stephens, but please call me Mia."

"Miss Mia. I've lived in this town all of my life. I've traveled to many places, even to your country of America. But this..." he waived his hand to gesture to everything around him, "this is a very lovely place. I think you may have been trying to write your paper for several days now? Yes?"

"Yes. Without much success. I've driven around and taken a ton of pictures. I've read nearly all of these books. Oh! You have a wonderful library here. But I've not met anyone except the lady at the local market, and she doesn't speak much English."

"Today is my last day to work this week, Miss Mia. If you would trust this police inspector, I would gladly take you on a tour of my city and tell you things those books probably do not mention. I have all day tomorrow to take you on a tour. Would that help you with your report?"

"Oh my, yes! That would be lovely. And who wouldn't trust a policeman?" she said shyly.

"An Inspector," he said to impress her. "Then shall we meet here again tomorrow morning? We can have our coffee and start the day."

"I will see you in the morning, Inspector Solberg. Thank you so much! Now that I have you, I finally feel as if I can make this a really good report." With that, she packed up her things and left. Inspector Solberg was quite excited about tomorrow himself.

The next day they spent the entire day together. He was a perfect gentleman as she soaked in much of what he told her. Even if she was fishing for any information that may help her in her plans, she actually had a pretty good day and decided that she didn't need to hate all men. The Inspector told her many interesting stories, even some police stories that were quite intriguing.

In an effort to let him feel as if he could tell her more secrets, she continued to indulge in her lie about being an American, telling him her father worked for the CIA. She alluded that she knew there were many agents in Europe, and that her father once told her he worked in Norway for several months, which was why she came to Norway to write her paper. Her father's stories were so alive and colorful that she just had to come see where he had been.

She looked at him very sternly and said, "Now you can't tell anyone that my father was CIA. You just can't. Promise me, Inspector. You have to promise me because I could get into real trouble."

"Of course, my dear, of course. I won't tell anyone. But I will share with you a few things about the CIA that your father may already know. And you, Miss Mia, must promise me not to write these things in your report. You can keep this knowledge to yourself."

Luna's plan had really come together at that moment. The Inspector spilled what could be the best information. Better than what she even thought she was looking for. She spent the next two days with him just to be sure he hadn't left anything out. So when the time came, she would know exactly what would need to be done.

The tram doors shut and lurched forward, bringing her back to the present moment. There were only five people on the tram, all of them sitting in front of her. She chose the back seats for a reason. She opened up her bag and put on the uniform over her existing clothes. She pulled the .22 from the bag, stuffing it down the back of her pants. She couldn't attach the silencer just yet or it wouldn't fit behind her back, so she shoved that in an inside pocket of her windbreaker jacket. She looked at all of the other passengers. No one was paying attention to her. She reached into her bag, pulled out the red wig and put it on. In less than twenty seconds, she looked like a new person. The tram was slowing down at the stop she knew Daniel Southerland would be headed. He was headed right for her.

Chapter 28

Daniel was now driving quite fast through the streets of Oslo, and Sonja was becoming more frightened by the second. "How ya doing back there, babe?"

"Danny. You just get us all to the hospital in one piece. Okay? I'll just try to not act as scared as I really am."

"You hang in there." He replied calmly, until he heard the distinct sound of metal-to-metal plink. He could hear the bullet ricochet off the side of the car. Knowing she was in the back seat actually made him feel as if this was the safest place for her. He installed a thin metal plate behind the back seat, covering it with the same cloth that lined the trunk so Sonja wouldn't ever see it. He quickly figured out that the small caliber bullets wouldn't be reaching her anytime soon unless it broke through the windows.

"Keep your head down, love. They seem to be getting a bit ugly with us." Daniel made a few more quick turns and started heading back toward the hospital. He was hoping that he could at least get into the hospital parking near the emergency room. Certainly they wouldn't be shooting at them right in front of the hospital.

Daniel's concentration on the black sedan had him start wondering just who was shooting at him. He hadn't heard or seen anything about the White Witch in several months. He was hoping she had totally gave up on them or someone else had killed her. That would be the best option, but it was just conjecture. He noticed the sedan was of the same model he normally used when he was on assignment - he could also see that the driver behind him was dressed as he usually would be if he were tailing someone. This didn't make any sense to him.

What if Stack lied to him? What if his boss had added him to some sort of list to eliminate him? Daniel hadn't crossed over to the enemy side. He didn't really work for Hugo. He was spying on him for the CIA. He was doing his job. Sure, he married the bad guy's daughter, but he didn't get married to his business! Daniel's thoughts were running rampant. What the hell was going on?

The more he concentrated on his driving, the more intense it became. He suddenly noticed another black sedan, but this time it was coming straight for him and the one behind him was very close now. The street he was on was covered with parked cars on the left and a sidewalk on the right. He was definitely being boxed in as he contemplated his next move. Then he saw the man in front of him aim a gun out of the driver's window.

"Hold tight, honey!" Daniel said and quickly turned the wheel right then left. This was the maneuver he was taught to use to change lanes at a high rate of speed without losing control of the vehicle. But this time he was forced to drive up on to the sidewalk. The bullets ricocheted off the front windshield and along the side of the car. He counted five shots. The first shot created a large spider web of cracks starting near the very top of the windshield. He breathed a sigh of relief as he was sure that if it had struck a few inches lower, it would have penetrated the windshield and hit him in the face, killing him instantly.

Daniel found a bit of relief when he saw that the sedan must have been the recipient of a few of those well-placed bullets. The car in his rearview mirror had a bullet-hole in the windshield. Daniel witnessed the vehicle slam into the back of a small flatbed delivery truck that he had just passed. The driver must have somehow hit the brake before being shot as the front of the car dipped just enough that it slid under the back of the flatbed, lifting the truck off the ground. The windshield was smashed and the flatbed was now directly over the driver's seat. The elimination of this pursuit took place in less than two seconds and Daniel turned his attention back to the road in front of him.

"Dammit!" he thought to himself just as Sonja let out a short scream. She had braced herself as best as she could. The stout Mercedes he loved so much was getting all scratched up, and Daniel was getting a more than pissed off. He could see his path narrow now that he was back on the road. There were cars parked on the right side of the street, and the black sedan was about to cut off his only path out of this mess. He shoved his right foot to the floor, gunning the engine, while downshifting manually. His heavy mass of metal pushed its way between the black sedan and a small red Fiat. His eyes locked onto the driver in the sedan, and in a surreal slow motion, he memorized his the face of the other driver. The black sedan bounced off the Mercedes, but then Daniel quickly found this driver was no novice. The man in the black tie used the momentum of the car, swinging the rear of the car around by spinning the wheel and stepping on the gas. The car did a complete 180-degree turn and was back in the chase in no time.

Daniel raced through a few more blocks until he could see an entrance to the highway. He quickly took that entrance and began to think of how he could get to the hospital before the man behind him could catch up.

Using the radio, the well-dressed assassin behind Daniel radioed his position. Daniel had no idea he was driving as fast as he could directly towards the White Witches' third black sedan.

Chapter 29

Now, traveling above the posted 110 kmh is pretty common on most major thoroughfares. Norway isn't much different in that respect. But as a whole, Norway has some of the safest drivers in Europe. Daniel couldn't seem to shake the car behind him. He had taken several high speed courses with speeds over 100 miles per hour back in Virginia, and he was beginning to think this guy had taken the same damn course. The speedometer was tipping 165 kmh or just over 100 mph, and Sonja was about to have a fit.

"Daniel! You need to slow down. I realize somebody is chasing us for no reason again but I don't think I need to be having this baby in the backseat of a car going so fast!"

Just about the time Sonja finished her sentence, Daniel spotted another black sedan driving much slower than the surrounding traffic. Even with his increased speed, he could tell this car was waiting for him to catch up.

"I think you're right, babe. I'm just going to slow things down a bit. How are you doing back there?" he asked as if he really cared, but he was really checking her mental attitude.

"I'm okay, but let's get to the hospital. You're about to be a daddy." She winced when she said this and Daniel's adrenaline pumped up again. He could see the beads of sweat showing up on her forehead.

During his excitement, the car behind had found its way to the outside lane, passing several cars and was now in his driver's side mirror. It only took one time for the black car to hit the left rear quarter panel just behind the wheel, causing the Mercedes to spin around. At this speed, Daniel couldn't spin the steering wheel fast enough and turn into the spin to straighten it out. The Mercedes hit the concrete divider and flipped over on to the driver's side.

The other cars on the highway began darting away from the wreckage, with several of them colliding, causing a massive traffic jam.

Inside the Mercedes, the only sound Daniel concerned himself with was Sonja's screams. Her seatbelt had caught her just right. She was actually standing on the side door handle and staring at the highway sliding by just under the window. She was also screaming at the top of her lungs. She had now hit her personal panic mode. Daniel was as calm as he could be assessing the entire situation. He was also stuck in the driver's seat. He quickly cut the seatbelt with his pocket knife and stood up. He had to get her out of the car before the bad guys begin shooting again.

"Don't pass out Sonja! Whatever you do, don't pass out. Also, try not to have the baby right now!" He was speaking loud enough to get her attention but didn't dare look directly at her. He knew he would get the evil eye from her, and he needed to get them out of this situation fast.

Daniel jumped up from the driver's seat, making a mental note of any injuries. He looked into the back at Sonja and could see that she seemed to be in shock, but was otherwise unharmed. "That was a great landing on the door! But don't move, sweetheart, I'll be right back!" Daniel's head popped out of the passenger front door window that was already busted. He could see the black sedan had skidded to a halt and was stopped in two lanes of traffic. The driver was already out and walking toward the Mercedes with his pistol in hand. He quickly turned and saw the other driver getting out of his sedan, and he also carried a gun.

Suddenly he could hear the bullets just whiz past his head, with a few of bouncing off the Mercedes. The back windshield busted into thousands of pieces, and Daniel knew he had to make his next two shots count. He came up out of the Mercedes window, pointing his Sig .357 at the man who was chasing him. A .22 round had just busted the outside mirror right beside him, and then Daniel heard three rounds sound off just as he fired his weapon. Daniel's two shots were true as he hit center mass of the nicely-dressed man who had been chasing him. He quickly turned to find the other man who was standing about fifteen feet away, and noticed his weapon was also pointing at the dead man in the street. The stranger's 9 millimeter Beretta had also hit the same mark.

Daniel swung his gun toward him when the stranger threw his hands in the air and in plain English yelled, "Don't shoot! Holy crap don't shoot me!"

"Who the hell are you?" Daniel yelled, with his gun still trained on the man's chest.

"Agent McMillan! The station chief sent me after you when he heard about the shootings near your apartment. We've got to get you two out of here, Mr. Southerland." The man looked Daniel right in the eye and waited for Daniel to acknowledge him as someone safe.

"I don't know you so you better not be jerking my chain. My wife is about to have our baby so let's get her to the hospital."

"Yes, sir." McMillian put away the Beretta that Luna had given him. The .22 was still stuffed between the driver's seat and the console. He was instructed by the White Witch after the first two drivers drove off that he might need to trade weapons but only if the situation called for it. He made this last-minute decision to give the appearance that he was not with the other two, and it appeared it was a good strategy. He felt pretty sure that Southerland would recognize the same type weapon that had been pointed at him for most of the morning. Luna's plan to try and gain his trust seemed to be working out just as she said it would. Killing the other drivers was also part of the plan, but more importantly, Southerland had to see him do it.

Daniel knelt down and pushed open the leather sunroof. It was large enough that she could easily step out and onto the road. She looked at the sunroof with a bit of a thankful smirk on her face as she looked at Daniel.

"You don't hate it so much now, do ya?" he said with a grin. He grabbed her by the hand and helped her over to the waiting black sedan. She got in the backseat of this vehicle and stretched out. As they drove away, sirens could be heard in the background.

"Which hospital do you want to go to, sir?"

"Take us to the airport." Southerland gave him a knowing glance.

"Of course."

Daniel's hair raised on the back of his neck.

The remaining drive to the airport would be anything but uneventful. The Southerland couple was glued to the story that was being told by Agent McMillian.

"Agent Southerland. You need to listen to me very carefully. Your boss, Agent Stack, sent me here to Norway to help you finish the job." McMillan looked over at Sonja via the mirror.

"It's called a marriage. She knows everything. Keep talking. I don't have anything to hide from my wife."

"Yes, sir. Stack says you've provided enough hard proof over the past few months to shut down the operation and to put Hugo away for good. Stack has been in touch with the State Police here and they have agreed to a joint raid. There are two teams that will converge at the restaurant to make the arrests. He wants you there as a family member and he will have you arrested, too, so you can maintain your cover. Once the three of you are separated for questioning, you will be cut loose and will be able to take your family to the U.S."

"I've always wanted to go to the U.S., Danny." Sonja gave him her two cents worth knowing she wouldn't have much choice.

"I think you would like New York.," he replied, squeezing her hand.

"But all that is tomorrow. Right now we have bigger problems. The pain in your ass with the white hair is onto you. Somehow she found out that you two were about to have this child soon and she made some phone calls to Nicklaus's group. I had just been inserted into his system just a month prior to your arrival in the country. I'm not even sure they trust me yet, so I volunteered for this assignment. I'm sure it will be the end of me in that organization, but I wasn't the only operative they planted. I'm supposed to take the both of you right to her or kill you on the way if you give me any problems."

"Wait. You're taking us to the airport, right?"

"Yes, sir."

"So she knows we have a medical base there? How the hell did she know about the CIA's hospital under Gardermoen airport? That's classified information."

"I don't know, sir. But she specifically told me that you be asking to go there."

"Damn, this lady is well informed."

"She's no damn lady, either." Sonja said quite annoyed. "She only wants to kill us! Did you ever stop and think of that?"

Sonja's comments kept popping out of her mouth. "Why can't you just let us go and you tell her you took care of us?"

"That would mean taking your left hands to her, along with pictures of your dead bodies. While I admire your thought process, we don't have enough time to just pretend you're dead." McMillan was blunt, but he was also right.

Daniel ignored her statement and squeezed her hand again for reassurance. "Well, Mr. McMillan, let's talk about how you're going to kill us before she does." Sonja's eyes just widened.

"You mean the White Witch, right sir?" McMillan was clarifying between the assassin and Sonja just to be sure.

"Yes. Wait. What did you call her? " Daniel said questioning if he really heard what McMillan just said.

"That's what everyone has been calling her. The White Witch. From Nicklaus on down, everyone is afraid of her. Several months ago she took out his top three men right in front of him and didn't bring a weapon with her. She's very deadly, sir."

"This I know."

"Don't let the corny comic book name fool you. She is very set on taking you out, ma'am."

"Me!" Sonja's eyes shot up to look at him in the mirror. Daniel's left eyebrow shot up, too.

"I thought this was some enemy of Danny's. What did I ever do to her?" Sonja was totally confused, and Daniel was trying to fit the pieces together.

"I have no idea, except that you are Hugo Henie's daughter. She said that no matter what, you have to die, and the husband is just for fun."

"Daniel! What am I supposed to do? What about the baby?" Sonja's voice had risen higher and she was scared as hell.

"McMillan, what about our baby. She knows we're pregnant." Daniel glared at McMillan and McMillan glared back without an answer. He couldn't bring himself to tell her the child would be lost, too. Daniel could feel the tear begin to form in his eye at the thought of losing his family. He could also feel Sonja's hand tighten around his.

"What are we going do, Danny?" she said in a quiet and panicked voice.

Daniel thought about his next words for a minute.

"You will do exactly as we say and everything will turn out fine." Daniel had already begun formulating a plan. "McMillan, how much time do we have until we reach Gardermoen?"

"About 20 minutes, sir."

"That will have to do." The black sedan raced toward the hospital ~ and the assassin. Daniel sat holding his wife's hand, planning strategy with Agent McMillan, a man he really didn't know but had no choice but to trust. For now anyway. He had no time and no way to contact his boss. His stress level had just about reached its maximum. He hadn't ever heard of any CIA agent who had to protect his ready-to-deliver pregnant wife from an assassin who was willing to kill everyone in their way...and him just for fun. This is probably why Stack was so pissed when he got married to her.

They spoke in detail, hoping they thought of everything. Daniel was even planning on how to deal with McMillan in case this was all part of "The White Witch's" plan.

McMillan drove to the multi-level parking garage. He chose the lowest level as Luna had instructed him to do, parking the car in space 17.

Chapter 30

Luna stepped off the tram at Gardermoen Airport. She walked through the terminal toward the northwest end. She knew exactly where to go as she had been to this station several times in her past. She didn't know then that the airport housed a full medical facility and living quarters seven stories beneath the runway.

Gardermoen Airport remained a pivotal location for European and American operatives to hide, live and have access to medical treatment for quite some time. The transformation into what it is today started with Harry S. Truman being sworn in on January 20, 1945, as Vice President during the Roosevelt-Truman administration. The United States has already seen Truman extend his political prowess during his election to his previous office of Senator for the State of Missouri, when he traveled to several military bases, outraged at the rampant overspending in late 1940's. His term as Vice President was short-lived when 82 days later, on April 12, 1945, President Franklin D. Roosevelt suffered a brain hemorrhage. As President, Truman's stern political stance on foreign policy preceded him as he traveled throughout Europe and the U.S. He traveled to Europe for the Potsdam Conference which took place in occupied Germany. Several events took place that summer, including his first meeting with Joseph Stalin, who was rumored to have known about the atomic bomb months before Truman found out about it thirteen days into his presidency. President Truman stood in front of many dignitaries, rulers and elected officials, extending his right hand to make even stronger ties with our allies. Norway was no exception.

Norway was under aggressive attack by Nazi Germany in the 1940s, during which time the King of Norway was King Haakon VII, who refused to let Nazi Germany invade. With the advice of parliament King Haakon VII fled to London to set up the Norwegian Government in Exile. Five years later, King Haakon, the royal family and members of parliament returned to Oslo on the cruiser HMS Norfolk of the Royal Navy, just seven weeks after Truman became President. A welcoming and congratulatory phone call from Truman to the monarch spawned a new friendship. The bond between King Haakon and President Truman grew strong within the next few years. In a show of unity for the upcoming Winter Olympics in 1952, President Truman offered for the United States to finance the lengthening of the runways of the Oslo Airport, which were not long enough for the newer, larger airplanes to land, bringing a flood of tourists to the city. King Haakon welcomed the gesture by President Truman as it would help Norway's struggling economy. The country was clawing its way out of an historic depression, and the influx of money would be well received

The funds were sent, and construction of the underground hospital was built without public knowledge. All the construction crew cared about was that they were working and were well-paid, having been told they were building underground parking and storage for large airplane parts. Some of them speculated it could be future bomb shelters for Norwegians, so they kept their mouths shut.

Nine months later, the dirt work covered the underground hospital, and the lengthening of the runway began.

Luna had no knowledge of the history the facility, and she didn't really care. She only knew she was going to use this to her advantage. She wasn't sure it would be the last time, either. She looked into her bag for one last item in her uniform. She was in a bit of a panic when she couldn't find it. Seconds later, her fear abated as she found the small, plastic object, hidden in the bottom of her bag. She grabbed the name badge and clipped it on her uniform. The badge she had taken it from a worker she disposed of the night before would do the trick. She would have access to the elevators, medicine cabinets and surgical rooms which, in Mrs. Southerland's case, would be the delivery room.

She continued toward the northeast corner of the airport causeway, locating the double doors marked "Storage Levels". She walked through the doors and down a short hallway. The elevator doors were the largest made in the 1940's, and designated as "Service Elevator Only". She pressed the button and waited for the elevator doors to open. She entered the passcode to send the elevator down several levels to enter the hospital.

Once the doors opened, she was greeted by a guard who seemed as if he had the most boring job in the world. She flashed her badge and walked on by. She was relying on this guard to not really pay attention to the badge, but to rely on the passcode being the main sentry. For security purposes, the passcode was changed monthly. In all of its years of operating, the code sequence had never been repeated. Before it was changed, employees were given the passcode before the end of the last shift of the week. Operatives had to call into the system to retrieve the current code. Luna made her last victim give her the passcode just before she shot her.

Getting into this facility had been easy for her. She hadn't see any guns on the guard, but she figured he had one. She calmly walked down the hall to prepare for the anticipated arrival.

Chapter 31

McMillan stepped out of the sedan and looked around. Seeing no one, he opened the back door to help Sonja out of the vehicle. Daniel stepped out of the other side, but not before he reached over and pulled the .22 caliber pistol from beside the front driver's seat. He looked at McMillan who stared directly back at him and said, "Let's hope we don't have to use these again today."

McMillan nodded and Daniel stepped from around the back of the sedan to help with his wife. She was breathing a bit easier now, but he could tell the contractions were getting closer. Daniel announced, "Let's go have a baby, shall we?" Sonja smiled at his ability to be a sweet husband, not allowing his tough-man CIA training get in the way.

They began walking to the parking garage elevator, keeping Sonja footing in balance. She may have acted like she was okay, but Daniel knew that the trauma of being chased, surviving a car wreck and being shot at all the while being in labor could cause her body to react to all this excitement. He really had no idea just how "fine" she truly was.

They had walked about twenty steps when they heard a car door open. A young blonde female stepped from between two cars and began walking toward the elevator. She was dressed in a gray casual business suit with a white blouse, pulling a carry-all bag on the wheels. Her steps were quick and her head was down as if to hide her face. Daniel put his hand in his jacket, gripping the .22, while McMillan had ahold of his .357.

The lady's pace quickened. She started to trot to the elevator, quickly catching up to them. Daniel could see her left hand dragging her baggage while her right hand dipped into her purse. She was less than twenty feet away. A perfect distance for a small caliber pistol.

Always maintaining a calm voice in tense situations, he asked her a question, "Where are you traveling today?"

As soon as he started speaking, she was startled and let out a gasp. "Oh! Uh, I'm headed to Rome. I'm sorry, you rather gave me a start." She pulled her clutch from her purse and Daniel could see her plane ticket sticking out of the end.

"I do apologize. I always feel as if these parking garages are sort of dismal and spooky."

"So do I." She noticed Sonja's abdomen and asked. "How far along are you?"

Sonja lied. "Only eight months, but I feel as if I could have it any day now." About the time Sonja finished her sentence another car door opened just a few rows away. A man stepped out and pointed his gun directly at Sonja.

As McMillan was drawing his weapon, Daniel was already firing.

"Move right!" Daniel said loudly so everyone would run behind the large, cement pillar. The young lady who just walked up froze in her steps. McMillan grabbed her by the waste while still shooting. She was being dragged around like a rag doll. Her mind was totally in a fog. "This couldn't be happening to me!" she thought.

"Holy crap! Not only do we have a mother in labor, we also have a woman in shock!" McMillan said with a frustrated voce.

Daniel had Sonja moving backwards towards the elevator. Even though the pillar was still between them and the shooter, they still had to get Sonja into a delivery room.

The shooter moved around the back of several more cars, carefully positioning himself to be protected behind the vehicles, yet maintaining a line of sight to the elevator. Daniel felt like they were sitting ducks. He continued to shoot when he could see the shooter about to fire. He was conserving his ammunition since he wasn't sure how many rounds remained in the .22. There hadn't been time to remove the magazine from the weapon to count. Of course, there was still his own .357 in the back of his pants.

The shooter's strikes were getting closer, and Daniel's concern was increasing as debris ricocheted. Finally, the elevator door began to open and it was empty.

"Go! Go! Go!" McMillan yelled as both he and Daniel started shooting cover fire. The shooter ran across the garage between the cars as fast as he could, lining up in the middle of the drive. He took careful aim and fired. Daniel saw him running and fired the .22. The last round exited the chamber and the slide locked back. The gun was empty!

The four of them had scrambled into the steel box as Daniel's weapon was emptied. He had no more time. The shooter had perfect aim on Sonja, and he fired. Sonja started to scream as she closed her eyes. McMillan fired his weapon with his last round at the same time Daniel pushed Sonja to the side of the elevator. The bullet slammed into McMillan's chest as he stepped directly in the center of the elevator blocking Daniel and Sonja, knocking him to the ground. Daniel could see McMillan's bullet had hit its target right under his nose, and Daniel watched the lifeless body fall as the elevator door shut.

The young lady with them fainted. Daniel shook McMillan. The bullet had hit him in the right lung. If McMillan hadn't taken the bullet for him, Daniel would be dead.

Chapter 32

The elevator doors were closed and Daniel entered in the passcode, hitting the same buttons Luna had hit earlier that day. The elevator began to lower underneath the airport parking garage. When the door opened, Daniel began to holler for anyone to help. The guard at the elevator doors jumped up as if he was glad some sort of excitement had finally occurred.

Daniel barked orders for three gurneys, which arrived quickly, as well as a few emergency room doctors. Daniel explained the injuries. McMillan came first with a bleeding gunshot wound, so he was taken directly into surgery. McMillan was still awake, and Daniel said they would meet again soon, thanking him for his brave efforts. For a man he had just met, Daniel was hoping that McMillan would be a long-lasting friend.

The young lady no one knew was given a sedative so that she wouldn't wake up. She was taken to a waiting room until the parking garage was cleared and cleaned up, at which time they would put her back on the elevator, to the airport, and place her in a chair near her assigned gate. She would probably wake up late and wonder if she dreamed the whole thing.

Sonja was placed on a gurney, and the red-headed nurse wheeled her down the hall toward a different operating room. Several other nurses raced into the room to prep for the delivery of baby Southerland. Doctors walked quickly into the room, barking orders. Sonja was lifted onto the surgery table, and IV lines were strategically placed in her arm. She tried to remain calm, which was difficult in light of the day's events -riding in that dreadful Mercedes' back seat on bumpy roads, being shot at and the vehicle landing on its side, meeting an undercover CIA agent, and in less than half an hour, watching that agent take a bullet on her behalf. Not to mention seeing your would-be assassin being shot and killed less than fifteen yards away, all the while being trying not to deliver her baby until it was safe! This has been one helluva day!

Sonja lay on the table, sweat on her brow. Daniel demanded that he would stay in the delivery room. There was no way in hell he would wait in the hallway or waiting room on a day like this. Nurses came in and out of the room, hung bottles of IV fluid, and connected his wife to monitors to track of her heart rate and vital signs. Electrodes were also placed on her abdomen to monitor the baby's heart rate. Daniel stood beside Sonja's bedside holding her left hand. "Just concentrate on me, love. Keep looking at me, concentrate on my face, okay?" he said lovingly. Doctors continued to give orders, and the room was full of organized chaos. Luna stood at Daniel's.

"Don't worry, sir, we'll take good care of her." She smiled as she looked him directly in the eye. Why does she look like she knows me? She must be Miss Congeniality around here and just has that face. She had walked into the room with a sense of urgency. She grabbed the IV bag, taking it off one hook and placing it on another just to look like she had a job to do. Keeping her head down so no one in the room would ask her to perform a medical function, she gingerly grabbed the IV line, found the input valve and rubber cap. She didn't look around as she concentrated on getting her job done. She shoved the needle in, slowly releasing its contents. As soon as she finished the full dosage, she turned and left the room. She knew in less two minutes she will have succeeded in exterminating her target and the child. Hugo's bloodline will stop.

Chapter 33

McMillan's injuries weren't life threatening. The bullet had impacted his clavicle, shattering it into several pieces, which was the blow that had knocked him to the ground. The .22 doesn't carry much knockdown power, but when a sensitive bone area like this is damaged, it puts anyone down. Daniel was careful to check and noted that the round went all the way through. McMillan was writhing in pain all the way into surgery. He was also furious that he got shot. The doctors were telling him to calm down and that his gunshot wound would certainly heal. Although he would be in pain for quite some time, he would be able to return to work, and possibly remaining in the field. The news was encouraging, but it didn't make the pain go away any faster.

The medical team was calm as they performed their duties in the operating room. Gunshot wounds were their specialty, and McMillan was glad that they had made it into the elevator alive. The plan was that Luna would surprise them in the garage, but the woman who surprised them wasn't Luna. He would have recognized her, even if she were disguised. Luna was strikingly beautiful with white flowing hair. Even wearing a wig, she was unforgettable. He memorized her face while stood in front of her when she was dishing out her plan to kill Sonja. His concern now was where she might be. He knew his cover was blown. He had left the radio in the car in the garage, and Daniel had taken the .22, but he didn't care. He was happy he was able to save Mr. and Mrs. Southerland.

When he recovered, he would be stationed in another part of Europe or possibly back in the states. He loved to travel, and he most enjoyed being undercover. He was able to take on any character, living that life, knowing it would be for a short amount of time, maybe a year and rarely more than that. This was actually the shortest undercover job so far, and knowing he had infiltrated a known mafia-type of gang and being so quickly chosen to be a part of a hit was actually pretty impressive to his boss. It wasn't a salary increase that attracted him, and he never wanted to be a station chief. Bossing others around and staying cooped up in an office was not on his to do list.

He laid on the table, the pain still agonizing, but he knew this would pass. He surveyed the room, taking a mental note of everyone in the room doing their job when his face froze. His eyes locked on her face, and without any hesitation she pulled the trigger. She immediately shot everyone else in the room with her own silenced .22, completing the job and eliminating all witnesses.

Her job was done. In her mind, Daniel was lucky to have lived yet another day. She recognized he was a force whom she respected, which was why she wanted to look him in the eye while she was killing his new bride and child. Introspectively, she didn't realize until now how arrogant that move really was. His family was dead and so was the double agent. Killing everyone in that room would send a message to the CIA to not be so cocky. She had informants everywhere. Besides, Nicklaus would be happy, too. She would call him later and tell him that her sources were right.

She found a different elevator and pressed the button. The doors immediately opened. She stepped in and pressed the button for the main floor of the airport. Her pulse was a cool 58 beats per minute, and she didn't have a drop of sweat on her forehead. She calmly stepped off the elevator as a red flashing light was activated above the door. She grinned as she made her way to the front of the airport where she hailed a taxi and disappeared, leaving the uniform and wig sitting on the floor of the elevator. She was now going to finish Hugo.

Chapter 34

Daniel stood beside Sonja holding her hand. "Just concentrate on me and we will be fine," he said in his ever-calming voice. She smiled back at him as the doctors were just about ready to help her deliver.

"Danny, I love you," she said as Daniel wiped the sweat from her forehead. "And I you," he replied.

"I'm feeling sleepy. Why do I feel sleepy?" she said as her eyes fluttered.

"Hey Doc? Why would my wife feel sleepy while trying to have a baby?" Daniel began to worry. He had never heard of this happening. He wasn't a doctor, but he also believed no one could ever be asleep and deliver a baby. Something was seriously wrong.

Suddenly the monitors began to shriek. Loud, solid sounds. BEEEEEEEEEEEP! Sonja was flat lining - her heart had stopped.

"Doctor!" Daniel had now lost his composure. "Nooooooooo!" Daniel screamed so loud it could be heard all the way down the halls of the basement hospital.

"Get him out of here!" the doctor said sternly. The nurses led Daniel out of the room. Daniel's anger made him think of all the events that had occurred today. He knew that witch was after them, but he hadn't seen..... And that's when it hit him. The nurse who told him that they would take care of her today. THAT was the White Witch! How the hell did she get into the hospital? This was a secure place! Daniel's face was turning red with anger. His jaw was clenched tighter than his fists. He wiped the tears from his eyes as he ran down the hall towards the elevator, but saw nothing. "Where's the other elevator to get out of here?" he yelled at the guard who pointed down the hall to the opposite end. "Down and to the right."

"Lock this place down! Now!" he yelled back as he ran as fast as he could. He turned the corner and saw the sign for the elevator. The guard hit the panic button, causing red lights to flash in the hallways. All elevators were shut down and the emergency doors were locked. Extra guards stepped out from their living quarters, weapons drawn. Daniel could see the second elevator had already reached the main floor of the airport above them. There was no way to get to her now.

To say that Daniel's heart was broken was an understatement. The only girl he ever loved, his pregnant wife, was now lying dead on the surgery table. He didn't know how he would ever get over this. The only reason she was dead was that he hadn't adequately protected her. He felt guilty that he had brought this wonderful, beautiful girl into his dangerous world. The more he thought about it, the more anger and remorse he felt.

As he rounded the corner heading back to the surgery room, one of the nurses said, "Mr. Southerland. You need to come in here." Daniel walked into the room where a nurse was holding his child.

All wrapped up in a warm blanket was his beautiful baby.

"She's a girl, Mr. Southerland." The nurse said proudly.

"I..I..I don't understand." He stood there in shock. "I thought. I thought..." he couldn't finish his sentence.

The doctor came over and explained that whatever the cause of death, the pregnancy was still viable if the child could be delivered quickly. The Cesarean operation was the only option. He expressed condolences for his wife as he explained his thoughts.

"Your wife may have suffered from anaphylaxis. We heard a little of what happened earlier today. We heard from the nurse who spoke to Agent McMillan. She had stepped out of his room after hearing the story of today's events. We're sorry about losing him too. But we think the stress of everything has contributed. She was simply overwhelmed."

"The nurse who was in here earlier, she had red hair and a China doll like face. She injected the IV with something. What was it?"

"We've taken blood samples and sent them to the lab, but whatever it was, it did not affect the babies."

"The babies?" Daniel looked at the doctor with confusion just as the nurse stepped around to Daniel's side. There, in front of him, wrapped up in a warm pink blanket was his second child.

"Congratulations, you have twins!"

Chapter 35

Present Time for Detective Sam Ackerman

It was time to find out more about the late Cindy Southerland. Sam knew Michelle was fairly new to the department, but not so new at research. He was fairly impressed by the young lady's work, but he didn't always show it. He appreciated her knack for discovering little details. Sam picked up the report and looked at Michelle.

"You should know that this file was very hard to get. I had to use our government contacts and they actually refused to cooperate until I spoke to an Agent Stack. There was no doubt that he knows more about this file than anyone. You and I are the only two who have clearance to read this, boss."

His eyes were asking if there was any pertinent information in the file. Michelle said, "Read the file, boss. It's in there." He grinned at Michelle for simply knowing what he wanted. Glancing down at the file he read the big red words "EYES ONLY". Walking away, he spoke over his shoulder, "Good work 'Kiddo'."

Sam walked down the hall realizing this file was more than just some light reading.

Born on April 8, 1990, near Oslo, Norway at Gardernoen Air Station. The record shows her mother died during childbirth. The father died in a military training accident the following year. Eventually, she and her identical twin sister were put in the adoption system when no other family could be found. Unfortunately, through very difficult circumstances that are fully described in their history, they were adopted to different sets of parents. Who, in their right mind, would separate twins, he thought. The sister's name is listed as Kathleen Lee Southerland.

Sam used his ancient and crappy computer to start a search. An old pc recently upgraded to Windows7, the processors could not keep up with the system upgrade. Plus, the department wouldn't cough up any money for flat screen monitors so the CRT monitor sat on his desk taking up unnecessary room. Daily he considered knocking the thing to the floor just to get a new one. He entered the victim's information into AFIS, the Automated Fingerprint Information System, pressed "Enter", and walked away, knowing it would take a while. The department had limited funds, and apparently the powers that be thought computers were not a necessity. Sam asked Michelle to keep an eye on the search results and to let him know when something showed up.

Sam called the garage to ask about his car. He wasn't happy with that conversation. Slow computers was one thing since he didn't even want to use them anyway, but he needed his car. Simpson and Michelle were working a few other cases at the same time, which was standard practice. All he could do now was to wait. He didn't like waiting when time was critical in cases such as this. He walked out of the station and down the block until he reached "Hank's", a local cop bar that had been around for just about as many years as the police station itself. Sam sat down in his usual place, glancing at the clock. 11:50 a.m. The bartender knew the drill for that hour of the day and promptly poured a glass of sweet tea. Freshly brewed, not that store-bought crap. The owner of the bar, Pauley, was as close to family as anyone else in Sam's life. His dad had been a cop many years ago, having been killed in the line of duty - a 9mm ricochet off the side of a building that caught him in the head. He didn't die instantly, but couldn't survive the surgery. Pauley decided to use his dad's insurance and what little inheritance he received to open up the restaurant in honor of his dad. Several of the townspeople who heard of Pauley's wish actually pitched in to help him buy the current location. Renovation costs were also provided by an anonymous donor, so Pauley's life was nearly set up for him when he was only 20 years old. Having a natural talent for cooking, he studied new management techniques, which resulted in Hank's Grill &

Bar being successful. Over the years, Pauley added a small music stage, complete with lights and sound system, for the weekend crowd and late-night cops. When live musicians weren't performing, he piped in some light jazz or something from the Rat Pack. Pauley had an old soul, which is why he and Sam got along so well.

Sam tapped his watch when looking at Pauley so Pauley jotted down Sam's usual lunch order and passed it over to the kitchen, putting a rush on it - a BLT sandwich. If it were after 6 pm, he would have had a ribeye, cooked medium, since a well done steak was way too chewy, and rare was just too damn cold by the time you got to the last bite. The steak would be topped off with caramelized onions and mushrooms and accompanied by a dark beer, usually Shiner. Sam treated himself once a week as he considered this to be his only vice.

As Sam finished lunch and his second glass of sweet tea, his cell phone rang. "You won't believe this, but I found her. She's here in the city, boss. You should head to the hospital. She's broken up pretty badly." Michelle said.

Chapter 36

Kathleen looked up from the hospital bed when Detective Ackerman walked in. Michelle's search found a police report from yesterday. There was a two-car collision just four blocks away from the deceased's residence which included Ms. Southerland's name. How could that be if she had just bled to death?

"Excuse me. Ms. Southerland? I'm Detective Ackerman." He said as he took off his hat.

"Finally! What took you so long? That guy who hit me, did you catch him? He slammed into me like he saw a ghost. What the hell?!"

"Excuse me…"

"The son-of-a-bitch just slammed into me. I thought he was trying to kill me. He jumped out of his some nasty ass beat up Bronco…"

He calmly interrupted, "Excuse me. Wait, wait, wait. Listen, Ms. Southerland, I'm not here about your wreck."

"Then what the heck do you want?" She was obviously agitated, and her pain meds were wearing off from her broken leg. He noticed bruising on both arms and her right jaw. Probably from the accident.

"I'm here about your sister, Cindy."

"Well of course you are! It's always about Cynthia! I'm so sick of this! Everyone asks about her. Well here it is: No! No, I won't introduce you. I won't get something signed for you and I won't give you her number! Now get the hell out and find out who nearly killed me!"

"Um, please Ms. Southerland. That's not it, either. But can you tell me the last time you saw her?" Sam could tell she was getting more agitated so he kept his voice calm.

"Yes. About an hour before my accident! What the heck is this about?"

"I'm not sure what the doctors have told you. Do you know that your accident was yesterday? You've been knocked out all night long." He said.

"Yes. I know. So who hit me? And what about my sister?" she insisted.

Sam ignored the first question and decided to answer her second. "Ms. Southerland, we got a call to your sister's home. I'm very sorry. Your sister is deceased."

Sam wasn't sure what her reaction would be. As far as he was concerned, she just yelled at him for walking into the room. She was not as banged up as Michelle told him. Her lungs weren't damaged at all. Yelling at the messenger was certainly a valid first reaction when someone was either guilty or couldn't believe the news.

"You're lying! I just saw her and she was fine!"

Maybe she wasn't lying, he thought.

"I'm so sorry." He said very calmly, hoping he would calm her down by speaking more quietly. He tilted his head toward the floor but never let his eyes off her. Most cops just say they are sorry because they think they are supposed to make some attempt at being sorry. But Sam's nature was such that he really valued life and any senseless loss of life was truly troubling to him. She could tell he was sincere. She yelled a few more times, but Sam didn't respond. Her demeanor began to change.

Softly she whispers, "Oh my God. No, not her." And the tears began to fall.

Sam took a few more steps toward her bed. He grabbed the back of a nearby chair, pulled it closer to sit down. He was about to ask about the last time they saw each other, but as she looked at him, he knew she wanted details. Her first question was not what he expected.

"Was her throat cut?"

Chapter 37

"Well..." no use in hiding anything here, he thought. She obviously knew something about this..."Yes ma'am. How did you know?"

"They said they would. They've been threatening for a while."

"Tell me, who are 'they'?"

"Voices on the phone. I...I have no idea who they are."

"You said 'they'. How many voices did you hear on the phone?"

"Two I know of. One man and I think one woman."

She was torn between emotions of guilt, anger and sorrow. Her tears kept coming. She was trying to stay composed but, understandably, failing miserably. Sam was patient.

"Why would someone be threatening her?"

"We don't know for sure. They never asked for anything, but they said something like, 'you got it all' and 'we gonna get it,' or something like that." She waived her hands in the air of if she couldn't remember exactly what was said.

"When did this start, Ms. Southerland?"

"About three weeks ago."

"Do you think it's someone you know? Someone close to you?"

"I don't know. Maybe, but I doubt it."

Sam stood up to make a call to Simpson. "Wait," she said. "Could you close the door, please?" Sam closed the door and came closer. There was something she hadn't told him.

"Detective. My sister was…" Suddenly the door pushed open and the nurse slightly leaned in the room.

"Sorry to interrupt. Just checking on you ma'am. Can I get you anything?"

"No," she said with tissue in her eyes wiping up tears. The nurse gave a cursory glance toward Ackerman and promptly left the room.

"You were about to say something." Sam politely prodded for information.

Even though it was just the two of them in the room, she motioned for Sam to scoot closer and she lowered her voice a bit - speaking with a cracking voice. "Detective Ackerman, it was Kathy they killed ….I'm Cynthia."

Sam leaned forward in the chair as if this was a story he really needed to hear. She explained how the media kept following her and wouldn't leave her alone. Recently there were paparazzi who were relentless to the point of stalking. She just knew that one of those damn photographers was following her day and night, waiting to catch some picture of her that would show up on social media in an unflattering way. She was fine with normal paparazzi when she decided to go out. That was just part of the lifestyle she lived. But when she was home or wanted to be left alone, there was still always someone watching lately. Then the phone calls started.

"I told my sister I really needed some time to think," she said. They decided to switch places for a couple days. The twins did this quite a bit since they found each other. They never got the chance to change places as kids. Kathleen never minded the attention. It was always temporary for her.

"I told her this was serious. She knew about the calls, Mr. Ackerman. She even heard one herself."

She told him everything.

"Why didn't you call the police?" he asked.

"That's where I was going when that guy hit me!" She started crying harder, knowing that she was too late in getting the police involved. Too late to help save her sister, her twin she shared everything with. The secrets, the laughs, the songs, the hugs....everything with Kathy was gone.

The door came open again. "Excuse me. Just checking on you," said the nurse.

"You guys are Johnny on the spot! Two nurses in two minutes. That never happens to me." Sam said.

"I'm sorry? I'm the only nurse for this patient, sir. My name is on that board right there." She pointed to the white board and held out her name badge. Sam darted out the door past the nurse, looking for the one who just left. He took the most direct route to the lobby, hoping she did, too. Brushing past nurses and patients in the halls, looking for any indication where she might have gone. But no sign of her. Sam began to make a mental picture of who he had just seen. A young, pretty brunette with a nurse uniform. Sam called Simpson and passed along what just happened.

Damn, he thought. *They know! They know they killed the wrong twin!*

Sam took the elevator back to Cynthia's room, regaining his breath and composure. He needed more information and he *had* to get Cynthia to a safe place quickly.

Chapter 38

With her leg in a cast and bruises still showing up, Sam was able to get Cynthia into a safe house rather quickly. She was still numb from the news of her sister's death. He had a protection detail outside. He would check on her when he could. He called and asked Ms. Mahalia to watch over Cynthia and they both agreed.

Sam found the investigator in charge of Cynthia's wreck to see if he had any leads on the man who left the scene. Officer Ben Brown said he was about to follow up on one. Sam said he'd like to join and would meet him in a few minutes.

Sam also called Michelle back at headquarters to correct the death certificate, but instructed her not to make it public yet. He didn't want the media to cause more problems. Michelle had more details about the knife that was used to kill Kathy. It was a ten-inch United Gil Hibben Survivor Bowie with a sawback blade and Micarta handle. The stainless steel knife was razor sharp on one side, while the back of the blade was heavily notched so one could cut thru a tree branch or saw through bone. The hilt of the handle has a protruding end that cups the end of the hand for a better ripping, sawing or cutting action. The Rambo-style knife may be intended for survival, but not Kathy's case.

Sam and Ben had worked several cases together over the years. They were partners for a short while before Ben moved off to help care for his father in Tennessee. He came back after his father died three years later. He could have stayed on at the small town police department of Bell Buckle, Tennessee if he wanted. However, when the population is posted as 1,502 everyone knows everyone and the Sheriff of Bedford County was plenty of help on a late Friday night when the cousins got out of hand. Not much really happened there and Ben was ready to get back to the big city.

Sam got in Ben's cruiser. It was clean, like his, and he wondered when he would get his vehicle back. Sam was curious and had several questions for Ben...until he got his first answer.

"Where are we going?" he asked.

"Beneath the city."

"Splendid. Just splendid." Sam was now on edge.

Of all his years of service, the Underground was the only place he had ever gotten shot. The scar on his right shoulder remained as a perpetual reminder when getting out of the shower of how fragile life is and how dangerous his job really can be. His daily prayer is that he would never have to return to where it happened. He already relived those memories enough to know that going back would really throw his senses on high alert. No one had caught his shooter yet, either. Two other officers died in the battle that day and Sam still thought there might have been more he could have done to prevent that. It wasn't his fault, but Sam took it upon himself to see that both families were taken care of properly. Those two deaths really haunted him. Ben was a bit apprehensive in telling Sam before he had gotten in the car. He knew Sam wouldn't turn back, but he also knew Sam avoided that part of town.

The Underground is a large place, dark, damp and smelly. These were old sewer and railway tunnels that were built when the city was growing. America's first subway system had three original tunnels: Boston Public Garden, North Station or Canal Street, and then the last one at Pleasant Street. Two of these entrances had been rebuilt or split up throughout the life of the city to allow for economic growth, expansion of the tunnels or to accommodate new trains. The last one, at Pleasant Street, was closed in 1962 when street car service came to an end. The entrance is now covered up by Elliot Norton Park. However, the tunnels remained and were now known as 'The Underground." Several more entrances had been found by indigents, or created out of necessity. Others were dug out during the depression by gangs so they could surreptitiously transport alcohol, tobacco and other items. For as many times as the authorities would try to clean out and close up these tunnels, they'd always been "reopened" and were still in use today.

These obsolete sections were still scattered with lights, and on occasion the electricity temporarily returned without warning. Cardboard cities were common, with homeless and hungry indigents trying to survive. Even without proper borders, authorities, or rules there is still a hierarchy amongst the bottom feeders. No one really knew the population, and most of those above ground didn't care. The subterranean passageways are sometimes hard to find. Some of the train tunnels lay on top of smaller tunnels that were so short that walking down the corridor required bending over at the waist. However, some of the tunnels intersected with old underground railway systems, and those were very noticeable, nearly impossible to hide in. These rat holes also have hundreds of vertical egresses that lead to alleys behind some of the best restaurants in town. Those who lived down there knew this town very well and which tunnels to avoid.

Ben pulled up near an intersection, got out and handed Sam a flashlight.

"Fresh batteries." He said and Sam nodded, not uttering a word.

Ben explained they were looking for a white male, approximately 26-30 years of age, 5'9, short dark hair and tattoos on his arms. Sam thought this would take all night, but prayed he was wrong.

Chapter 39

Smelly, humid and dark, Sam and Ben headed under 45th Avenue. A man fitting the description was seen running into the tunnel at this location. His white 1988 Ford Bronco with a smashed up left front quarter panel sat parked just a block away. An undercover cop working overtime was watching the Bronco. Sam and Ben started their search farther down, hoping to flush out the UNSUB.

They were nearing their exit when a group of three men jumped out from a dark corner and ran.

Ben was pushed down as two of them ran deeper back into the darkness of the Underground. Only one ran into the light.

"You go after that guy!" Sam said as he ran after the other. In the dark and without knowing the markings on the walls very well, Sam was aware that he was running into the same area where he was shot. He wasn't afraid to go back in, but there are a few things in life that just took some time to get over. His stomach felt queasy. This felt more like a trap than just a good lead. "What the hell am I doing!" he thought. "I'm heading back into a dark, smelly-ass tunnel with the light at my back chasing another stinkin' bad guy. Damn this job!" Sam reached up and tilted his hat to tighten it on his head, squinting his eyes to adjust to the darkness. "Here we go!"

Ben was slowly catching up to his UNSUB as he jumped over trash obstacles that were being pushed over in his path. His skills on the track team at the University of Alabama were working for him. The thirty extra pounds he gained after college were not. Barely catching his balance, Ben was just a few steps behind.

"Freeze!" he yelled. The UNSUB looked over his shoulder too late. Ben was already in mid-flight. He smashed into him and they crashed into the wet ground. Seconds later the unknown runner was cuffed and Ben was breathing easier until he heard shots fired.

Sam had chased his UNSUB through several dark corridors, around homeless people and over trash. Sam was pushing himself to keep up the pace. His mind was at work here and his senses were heightened. The UNSUB description fits! Sam ran his fingers through his ever-graying hair, and shoved his hat back on. He still looked ruggedly handsome, but he knew time was taking a toll on him. A few more wrinkles, a few more pounds, but the ladies were still chasing him from time to time. Time wasn't on his side right now. Shots whizzed passed him again. "Well, shit. That's another hole in my jacket. I'm getting tired of this!"

Sam looked out from his position behind a fifty gallon drum and yelled "STOP!" But there was no chance of that happening. The suspect ran around a corner and down to the next. He drew a 9mm from his waistband and waited for Sam.

'BANG!'

Immediately, Sam was spun to the ground, wincing in pain.

'BAM! BAM!' Sam returned fire as he lay out in the open.

Ben had called in for backup when he heard the shots.

'BANG!' Heat from the bullet whizzed past Sam's head.

Crap! He's a good shot, Sam thought as he scrambled for the corner of the next corridor. He sat on the ground in some sticky wetness thinking about the infection that could result, and he was not looking forward to a tetanus shot. Sam peaked around the corner, got up and took a deep breath and kept moving.

'BAM! BAM!' Sam dropped his clip into his left hand without a sound to not give away his position, and with precision shoved another mag into his gun; however, the echo of the tunnel couldn't stop the sound of the next round slamming into the chamber. More rounds came his way. Sam's eyes finally adjusted to the darkness as he continued to move in the damp corridor. This time he hugged a doorway that probably lead up to the surface. Sam looked across the tunnel and could make out a scared, shaking homeless woman. Sam put his finger over his lips to be sure she stayed quiet. She pointed her finger down the tunnel and up to the left. Sam nodded.

Sam made his way quietly to the end of tunnel and could see that it opened up into a large expanse with two levels. He could just make out where his UNSUB was waiting for him up on the left side. The high ground was better, but he had no escape, either. No exit doors could be seen. This was it. Sam knew that once these next few moments started, there was no turning back. No options left. He also knew he needed to take a moment to think about how this would play out.

"Throw down your gun, son. There's no way out of here. It's just you and me now, but more cops are on the way. There's no need for us to keep shooting at each other."

"Screw you, Ackerman!"

Sam's left eyebrow went up. How the heck does he know who I am? Must have been somebody I arrested before. All my friends don't play in this neighborhood.

"Who are ya, kid?"

"A bad memory." And with that he jumped up and began firing again. Bullets were released with a vengeance, but Sam had already moved position after his last question. Sam's two shots were true, hitting the man square in the chest.

The UNSUB fell. Sam's weapon stayed trained on his chest as Sam drew closer, jogging up the ramp. He kicked the gun away. Blood was spreading fast. Little time to spare.

"Why did you kill Ms. Southerland?"

Coughing, he sputtered, "Didn't...but...but..." Sam leaned in closer.

Ben and his suspect-in-tow showed up at the end of the tunnel. So did the curious homeless lady.

"What did he say?" Ben asked.

"Says he didn't kill Ms. Southerland, but he was the one who shot me...twice."

Sam knew his own shooting case was closed. His shooter lay in front of him from Sam's own bullets. He wasn't looking forward to writing this report. And, Cynthia's would-be killer had just slipped away. Sam was pissed and frustrated. His career had always been reactive to the clues and information. His actions were defensive. It was time to rethink that, and he was formulating a plan.

Chapter 40

Sam's arm was in a sling. The bullet went all the way through. He was sitting by Cynthia, explaining the previous night's events. A chemistry was developing between them over coffee. She was certainly beautiful on the commercials, but he found her so much more attractive just sitting in her sweats with much less make-up. Conversation was easy and unhurried. No pressure. She spoke of her adoptive parents and how she grew up without her sister. She was told about her twin a long time ago, but never expected to actually find her. Sam wondered who in their right mind would only adopt just one child, knowing they were twins, but he decided that's just another screwed-up government system and perhaps a conversation for another time.

Cynthia explained that Kathleen was the one who actually found her. Cynthia's (and Kathleen's) face was often seen on TV in commercials. Someone asked Kathleen when she had started doing commercials. Kathleen was confused by the question and asked why. She watched the TV a bit longer with her friend and there it was. A commercial with her face on it. Kathleen was never told she was a twin. She freaked out a bit, then blew it off. But a few months later after her 19th birthday, she looked up the actress on the internet. Same birthday. Same birth place. Different name. Apparently, adoptive parents can change the name of their adoptive child. But the resemblance and history were too much to ignore any longer. Kathleen went to a lawyer, going through all the proper channels, and sent a letter to Cynthia through her manager. They agreed to meet. Cynthia was so very excited, but Kathleen was very apprehensive. She was angry at her adoptive parents for hiding this from her. Anger aside, Kathleen's adoptive parents had divorced, and no one really spoke to each other once she moved out at 17. Her rebellion at her parents was the tattoo on the back of her neck, yet she kept long hair to cover it. Kathleen found new friends in her sorority at college. She started going to church and singing in the choir, but was never one to bring attention to herself. She didn't have many boyfriends, either, which was why she didn't mind taking Cynthia's place from time to time. She could pretend to be famous for a bit and then disappear back into her life where she was just a face in the crowd.

Cynthia filled her in on how their lives were so different. Cynthia's parents were totally involved. Her adoptive mother was a teacher and was very active socially. Cynthia also sang in the church choir since she was little. She was the life of the party no matter where she went. Once they got to know each other, they became close sisters. They hung out when they could, but that wasn't enough for Kathleen. She packed up everything and moved to town to be closer to Cynthia. It was Cynthia's idea for Kathleen to pretend to be her every once in a while. She wanted to give Kathleen a taste of being in the limelight. While it wasn't too often and never in a really important shoot, they never got caught. Until now.

Chapter 41

Ben filled the Captain in at headquarters and was officially assigned as Sam's partner. No matter how hard they tried, the media still found out about Kathleen, but hadn't found the safe house yet. Ms. Mahalia hung around and helped out as needed.

Sam and Ben were out of clues. They started over from the beginning. Sam filled him in on everything. He had tough cases before, but this was becoming a little more. They discussed the case for several hours until Sam was tired. Then he prayed.

Cynthia was already asleep on the couch. Ms. Mahalia brought Sam some tea. Two sugars, of course.

Ben stepped out for a phone call. "Yeah Michelle, what's up?" he asked.

"Is Sam with you?"

"Yes. But he's sacked out, exhausted. Could be some of the medication making him tired."

Michelle explained the bumble with the records the first time as some computer mix-up and closed adoptions processes. But she finally got to the good news.

"You ready for this? Sam is a genius. He asked me to check out the crime scene to see if this could be a serial killer. I thought it was a weird request, but Sam has a knack for this stuff. So, remember the knife in the ceiling?"

"Sam told me about it."

"That's the oddest thing. Lots of cases have a murder weapon similar to this model blade, but I did find just one who left it in the ceiling."

"Keep going."

"Four years ago, in Chicago, a 22-year old was in a scuffle in an apartment. Three guys and one girl involved. Two of the guys testified against the third. The report indicated a struggle between two of the guys. Somehow the girl got in the middle of it, ending up as the victim. He cut the girl's throat and left her for dead, but she survived. The other two guys were cut but they ran from the scene before the girl was injured. It also states the UNSUB had cuts and stab wounds on him, too. The two who ran were caught since the screams were heard by the neighbor and the security camera caught them on video running by the convenience store down the street. Eventually, all the circumstantial evidence and the two testifying against him did the trick. He got two years for aggravated assault with a deadly weapon. He served a year-and-a-half. He's been out for about three years now. He fits our description. His name is James Traylor."

"Chicago, huh? I'll call over there to see if we can get an address for him. Thanks."

"Not so fast. I'm new at this but I'm not without my own resources. I've already called Chicago. He's not there anymore. Are you sitting down?" Her question was rhetorical. "Traylor lives right here now according to the Driver's License Bureau."

"Dang, girl. You're as good as Sam says you are. Thanks. Call the Captain and I'll tell Sam."

"Thank you, but you are too late. I have already called the Captain. And Traylor's information was sent to both Sam and your cell. Oh, and you are most welcome."

"Amazing." Ben hung up and quietly woke up Sam and pulled him outside the room so not to wake Cynthia.

Ben gave Sam all the details. Sam was groggy but this break provided a renewed sense of purpose. A new lead.

Unfortunately, a call to the Captain to see if more men could be used to help with the case was to no avail. Ben and Sam were to do this alone. The department was stretched too thin.

This time the duo climbed into Sam's car which had been brought to Sam just an hour ago. Cleaned up, didn't smell like smoke and with new brakes. "Small victories," Sam thought but glad nonetheless.

The afternoon sun was bright when they pulled up to the suspect's house listed with the DMV. Sam's good arm was ready to draw his weapon if necessary. Just as in the past when they worked together, their gestures and communication fell into place like old times. Sam was actually glad to have Ben back in town.

Sam took the front door while Ben quietly went around back.

Sam rang the doorbell. He heard steps and the door opened slowly.

"Hello," she said. "May I help you?" She was short and fluffy like Sam's grandmother, gray hair and all.

"I hope so. I'm Detective Ackerman. I'm looking for a James Traylor. Does he live here?"

"Oh, no. He's my grandson. He doesn't stay here. Is he in trouble again?"

"Well the DMV has listed this address for him. May we come in?" Sam asked politely while his eyes surveyed his surroundings.

"Of course, Detective."

Sam texted Ben the usual coded "**" which translates to be alert, and join him when he is ready.

"What's your name, ma'am?" Sam led the conversation.

"Janet Traylor Ross," she said.

"How long have you lived here, Mrs. Ross?"

"Oh, round about forty years I believe."

"Have you seen James recently?" Getting to the point.

"Well, about three days ago, he came to the house in a big white truck. It was very loud and I told him so. He's been in and out of here since he got out of prison. That's why he has an address listed here. Since my husband died six years ago, I haven't had any company in the house except for James. The system wanted him to stay with family, but I couldn't make him stay put. He just doesn't stay long, mind ya. But, I do keep a room for him upstairs with the hopes that he will return. He is the only family I have left."

"Mind if we look around a bit?"

She shook her head and Ben cautiously began searching the first floor. When that was done, he started up the staircase.

"What kind of trouble is that boy into?" she asks.

"The kind that makes grandparents sad, Mrs. Ross." Her heart sank. Her emotions were easily seen.

Ben came downstairs. "Found these, Sam." He produced a pair of earrings and a pawn ticket. Earrings such as this weren't even the kind that men would typically wear, and the pawn ticket had the date of the accident on it. Ben was pretty good at working a room.

"Are these yours, ma'am?" Ben asked Mrs. Ross.

"No, sir. Haven't ever seen them before. I don't really poke around except to gather up the laundry," she replied.

"Does James wear white shirts, Mrs. Ross? The type that button up the front?"

"Not usually. But he does have one. I know since I'm the one who bought it for him to look nice for the judge the last time he screwed up. Hold on. I'll go see if I can find it." She said as she stomped up to his room. Ben followed.

Sam began to look around the modest room. Pictures of her family hung on the wall. A cross over the counter gave Sam some hope. The place was clean and tidy. It appeared as if she was a good, old-fashioned grandma trying to help a lost grandkid, but she wasn't having much luck.

"I'm sorry, Detective. It's just not here," she said to Ben.

They returned downstairs. Sam closed the conversation with the usual pleasantries, gave her his card and left. As they walked off the porch, a white beat-up Bronco was parked down the block about 200 yards.

"Do you see the Bronco down the street to the right?" Sam asked.

"Yep. Isn't that listed as the vehicle that hit Cynthia?"

"I believe so. I knew I liked working with you."

"Hell yeah. Let's get in the car - you know we're about to chase him." Ben said.

"Yup."

"Besides, you're a busted up ol' man today." Ben nodded to Sam's arm.

"Trust me. I'm about to show you that a busted up ol' man can still get the job done."

Chapter 42

The second Sam started the car Ben turned on the "red and blues", and as the lights flashed, the tires on the Bronco began to smoke against the pavement and started backing up as fast as possible. Ben called in the chase to the dispatcher. Sam's driving skills were slightly impaired with his arm in a sling, wincing several times but doing his best not to show any weakness to Ben - he would never live it down. They sped through the narrow streets at nearly 60mph now. The older neighborhood was filled with cars parked on the street. Sam hated these neighborhoods just for this reason. The fire department hated it worse because it was difficult to get their trucks through without damaging cars. These narrow streets should be a one-way.

The Bronco was using maneuvers trying to shake Sam, but Sam held his own. A turn to the right had Sam's car fishtailing across some loose dirt and the Bronco seemed to be losing them.

"Take the next right, Sam!"

"What?!"

"Turn right, Sam. Now!"

Sam yanked the wheel and the Chevy fishtailed again, grazing the curb and just missing a fire hydrant. Sam trusted Ben but gave him the evil eye for not getting more of a warning.

"What? I just recognized this part of town. Your suspect is about to hit a dead end. Take a left up here."

Sam flung the car left and there was the Bronco headed right at them. Holy Crap! Sam skidded the car to a stop. Both he and Ben jumped out as the Bronco had nowhere else to go as it smashed the driver's side of Sam's unit. The Bronco flipped over as it flew in the air. Pieces of the Bronco whizzed past Sam's head as he dove behind another car. The glass from one of the cars went shattering toward

Ben, slicing his face and torso like shrapnel. He cried out and rolled to a stop.

They both looked toward the Bronco as it landed upside down. The top is crushed and they couldn't see in. Sam was standing first, weapon drawn. His left arm was screaming at him. As Ben struggled to get up, his blood was soaking through his shirt. He shook off the buzzing sound in his ears and reached for his gun, but it wasn't there. He searched the area and saw it about forty feet away. He ran for it as James Traylor smashed into him.

Ben slammed into the asphalt as James ran for the gun. In seconds, Traylor had Ben's gun pointed at him.

"Sam!" Ben cried out, looking down the barrel of his own weapon.

"Freeze, Traylor!" Sam's weapon pointing right at Traylor while his voice is calm but direct. Sam stood as unflinching as a statue about twenty feet to Traylor's left. "Don't move, kid. Your grandma doesn't want to bury her grandson, and I don't want to be the one to tell her why. This is a no-win situation, James. Please put the gun down."

Sirens in the background were closing in. Traylor closed his eyes in hesitation. Sam put more pressure on his trigger and exhaled just as Traylor slowly lowered Ben's weapon before dropping it.

Ben laid his head on the asphalt, breathing easier and thankful that Sam just saved his life.

Traylor was in handcuffs in a patrol unit in no time. Sam's arm was bleeding again, but not enough to worry him. Ben had blood on him, too, and the paramedics had patched him up. No serious wounds, and he refused to go to the hospital. Sam was staring down the street for a moment as he saw residents coming out to watch. He looked at a little boy at the end of the block being pulled in a wagon. He remembered that his uncle used to pull him in a Red Flyer wagon when he was about three years old. Sam was a cute kid with a killer smile who learned how to wink on command. A girl magnet for his uncle. People were safer tonight, he thought. Ben caught Sam's attention and brought him back to the scene.

"Hey, Sam. Thanks for that, partner." No response from Sam. He just kept looking around. "Are you okay?" Ben asked.

Sam looked around again and saw the mass of crunched-up metal in the street, then looked directly at Ben. "You're welcome. But I'm so hacked off right now." Sam replied.

"What? Two gun fights in the same week get under your skin?" Ben says. "You certainly showed me how it's done. Even old and busted up."

"No. Not that. That's part of the job. I *just* got the brakes fixed. Next time we take your car."

Chapter 43

Forget the glass of water. The interrogation room is always hot and smelly. Long hours with too many cops and suspects have passed through that room. The Captain and Sam watched from behind the glass. This was Ben's specialty.

"How did you know the woman you killed?"

"I didn't kill nobody."

"We know all about your past, Traylor. It's public record, and what's not public I've got right here." He jams his finger on top of the one-inch file in front of him.

"What happened here?" Ben shows six or seven photos of Kathleen's murder scene.

"Looks like a fight to me." Traylor was simply glaring at Ben while cuffed. Ben would be asking as many questions as he could before James opted to "lawyer up".

"Yeah. A fight you had with her and she ended up dead."

"I told you I didn't kill her."

"Well, no one believes you. Heck, even your grandmother is upset with you. She thought you turned your life around."

"I did my time. I paid my dues. Why'd you go and get her all mad at me? You leave her outta this!" Ben struck a nerve.

Sam was thinking he knew Traylor. He seemed familiar somehow.

"This girl was murdered the same way you left your last victim. Except this time you succeeded! Ms. Southerland is dead. The D.A. is going for the death penalty, and with your past, it's a slam dunk. So tell us how this happened."

"I told ya. I didn't kill nobody. I don't know why anyone would kill Ms. Kathleen."

Ben stopped. He looked up into the camera to show Sam he noticed it, too. Captain Keener was also interested. He knew all the details.

"How'd you know this was Kathleen?"

"She gots that tattoo right there on her." He nodded to the edge of a photo barely showing the back of her neck.

"She don't really show it very much. Keeps it covered up," Traylor says.

Sam's eyes widened. He had just figured out the connection. He had seen James' picture on a wall just a few days ago. Why didn't he realize the connection earlier? "Call the safe house now, Cap! Make sure you talk only to Cynthia!" The Captain began calling immediately.

"So how'd you know about it?" Ben prods.

"She used to come over to Ms. Cynthia's every now and then. Especially when she had too much to drink and some dude with her. Ms. Kathleen lives way on the other side of town and Ms. Cynthia was downtown where most clubs are."

"How do you know where these women live, Traylor?"

"Cuz my girl do the cleaning. I go with her when I ain't working."

Sam's eyes grew wide. Confirmation! Traylor is Ms. Mahalia's boyfriend. "Any answer, Captain?"

"Nothing." He replied. Sam banged on the glass and Ben came out quickly. "Let's go!"

Chapter 44

Ben and Sam raced out of headquarters in Ben's car as Sam tried to call Cynthia. The call went straight to voicemail. Since there were two gun fights in this same case, the Captain told the Mayor to shove it and added some over time to the budget. Sam called the team out in front of the safe house. Again, no answer.

"Faster!" Sam yelled. He couldn't get there quickly enough. Certainly, the entire case was important, but his emotions were also ramped up now with this attraction to Cynthia. He knew this was brand new to both of them and couldn't tell where it was going, but that didn't make this any easier. "Drive, dammit!"

Sliding to a stop beside the unmarked unit, Sam jumped out of the passenger side. The cops outside were unconscious, one was bleeding. Ben radioed the Captain. Ambulance and backup were already on the way. Sam was already at the front door. He was frustrated that it hadn't occurred to him that Ms. Mahalia was in on it. How could he not have remembered that weird feeling he had when he first met her? He had to put that aside for now as Ben stepped up beside him.

Hand signals again. "3...2..." He held up one finger and pointed. They went in quietly.

The house was quiet. They worked briskly. Eyes and gun barrels darting everywhere. Every closet, every corner. Sam was hoping he wouldn't see another slit throat lying in a pool of blood. The first floor was cleared. At the last door on the left they went in. The last door was the basement. Sam hated basements. The stairs were too narrow and afforded no place hide in an ambush.

Sam pushed open the door and Ben stepped in first. They walked quietly down the stairs. Ben was nearly on the bottom step when he heard, "Don't move or she dies."

A lone female voice from the dark corner of the room.

"I'm Detective Ackerman."

"I know who you are. Stay right there and drop your guns."

Sam's eyes slowly began adjusting to the darkened room.

"Who are you? Why are you doing this?" stalling for time. He couldn't see her yet.

"Drop them now I said!" demanded the voice while giving away her position a bit more.

Sam bent down slowly lowering his .357 to the ground.

"Your buddy, too! Or she dies sooner!"

Ben slowly lowered his weapon, too, and dropped it on the stairs with his left hand.

Sam could now see Cynthia. Her hands bound behind her back. A long knife at her throat just like the one that killed her sister. Ms. Mahalia was on the floor, unconscious.

"She had the perfect life. The men, the money, clothes, paparazzi. And she stole it all from me!"

Sam's eyes could see better now. So could Ben's. The lone girl brandishing the knife was young and beautiful. Runway-quality type of girl. Her eyes were glaring at Sam with a hollow look of loneliness. She was missing something in her life and she couldn't take it anymore. Ben slowly lifted his suitcoat as he leaned forward. He reached out to Ms. Mahalia. They thought she was a part of this, but maybe they misjudged. He could tell she was breathing, but she was totally out.

"Let me help her."

"Don't touch her! Don't you move I said," she yelled.

"She's bleeding. She needs an ambulance." Ben was drawing her attention to him.

"Cynthia here is about to need an ambulance, but they won't be able to make it in time. She stole my life, her grand-daddy stole my mother's life and now I'm going steal hers!" The blade bit at Cynthia's neck. Tears coming down her face, fear in her eyes and now blood dripping on her neck.

"Wait! You already took her sister's life. She doesn't have anyone else." Ben was hoping to dig out a confession for killing Kathleen, and hopefully gain a glimmer of sympathy.

"The sister was collateral damage. Girl shouldn't be pretending to be someone she wasn't, and I didn't even know about her until a few days ago. And if this bitch's granddaddy hadn't been such a monster, this wouldn't have happened at all!"

Cynthia was confused; a worried look on her face. "I don't have a grandfather. I was adopted."

"Yes. That's what took us so long to find you." She grimaced. "Then when I found you, I didn't want to kill you. I thought you were my friend." Mia's voice got choked up a bit. She was agonizing about what she was doing. Her emotions were taking over ~ her eyes began to glaze over a bit and her voice turned to a harsh whisper, "But you stole my career! I don't have any friends now." And the knife started to cut deeper into her neck.

"I didn't steal your career, Mia." Cynthia said, crying as she felt the knife bite harder. "I tore up the contract from the modeling company when I found out they lied to BOTH of us! I told them they cheated you! You should have gotten that contract. I even changed managers after that, Mia! I didn't get any work until six months later. I even had my new manager call you about it, but they said you were gone." Cynthia was pleading now. "Please, Mia! It's not my fault, please." Cynthia was sobbing now.

"I don't understand, Mia." Sam said calmly. "Why were you trying to find Cynthia?"

"Little Miss Innocent here doesn't even know her family history. But I do! Her granddaddy, Hugo Heine, stole my mother off the street and sold her to the highest bidder! He did that to hundreds of girls! He was a monster. My mother was one of only a handful of girls who escaped, but she was definitely the only one who ever sought revenge. You don't have any parents since my mother killed them and it's my turn to finish it!"

Cynthia had never heard of this before now. She had no idea of any of this. As the knife cut into her neck, her eyes widened and she let out another shriek.

"I'm sorry!" cried Cynthia. "I'm sorry for all your pain, Mia. I never knew. I never knew any of this. And I'm sorry if I hurt you. Dear Jesus, I'm so sorry." Tears were coming out of Cynthia like never before and her strength was gone. She had no energy to fight back. She had resigned herself to the fact she was about to die.

Ben leaned forward a bit more, revealing his back up pistol in the back of his pants. A small Ruger LC9 sub-compact with Laser sites. He could only hope that Sam could see it and still watch Mia's hands. With two gun fights already on this case, Sam and Ben now carried three weapons each. Ben's third was strapped on his ankle while Sam had a Sig Sauer .380 Model P238 in a small shoulder holster hidden by his jacket. Ben could see Sam's .380 from his crouched position and thought about grabbing it, but he wasn't sure he could prevent Cynthia's throat from being slit. He was thinking this girl was surely about to die when he thought he could feel Sam cautiously lifting out the gun from the back of his pants.

Blood was flowing fairly easily down Cynthia's neck. Sam couldn't figure out if a major artery had been cut or if the blood was simply smeared in the struggle. He also knew he didn't have much time to find out. It appeared that Mia had cut deep enough that Cynthia's blood loss could cause her to faint before she died.

"No! You liar! It is your fault! I have nothing! Nothing because of your damn family and you! And it's time this is over!"

No negotiation. No thinking about the next move. There was only one move to make and there was no room for error. He would have to take the chance that might hit both of them and hope that damn ambulance would get here quick. Sam gently pushed Ben, who immediately understood, and moved out of Sam's way as the gun was pointed directly at Mia.

BAM! Sam's bullet hit the target. A head shot was the only option he had. No matter how hard Mia tried, her skills were not as good as her mother's.

Mia fell to the floor. Cynthia screamed and dropped to her knees. As she began to pass out, Sam caught her and held her close.

"It's okay. You're okay. I've gotcha. You're safe now. I gotcha." He said as Cynthia was out cold.

Sam recognized Mia as the first nurse from the hospital. She was lying there lifeless. She had ice blue eyes and porcelain skin. She was quite beautiful. He noticed her coal black hair with a single streak of white flowing across her face.

Details unraveled fast at headquarters. Seems Ms. Mahalia's two-year-old girl was in a car seat around the corner in the basement when all the lights came on. Mahalia explained her kid was kidnapped and she was forced to help the suspect gain access to the actress' home. Mahalia wasn't at the apartment when Kathleen was killed nor did she expect anything like that to happen, but she discovered Kathleen's death was no accident, if they had only known she had a twin.

Mia found out it was the wrong girl when Traylor said he just hit her with his Bronco. That didn't add up to Mia. Cynthia was dead. She did the job herself. She didn't know Cynthia was a twin. Most of the world didn't know, which was quite a bit of work considering what Cynthia did for a living. Mia found out as much information as she could about Cynthia and discovered her housekeeper had a bit of trouble with men. She watched Mahalia until she saw James Traylor. He was a fine specimen of a male and she decided to use her looks and see how far it would get her. Besides, men were the weaker of the two sexes in her mind. Show a little skin and give them a wink and they would do just about anything for a pretty face. She played Traylor for five months. Mahalia had no idea he was cheating on her. One drunken night Traylor bragged about the details of his time in jail when Mia got the idea to frame him. She planned it down to the smallest details. The cops would surely find the clue with the knife stuck in the ceiling. No one would ever know she was a cold-blooded killer.

Chapter 45

Eighteen months before Kathleen's murder

Mia picked up the phone and called home. "I've found her." She said smugly.

"I knew you would. Now use your beautiful face and get to be friends with her. You need to be patient, kind and fun. Match her personality. But never forget WHY you are doing this. She isn't a normal girl. She will eventually break. Her mind will snap. It's hereditary. Her grandfather was a monster. He was a mastermind in human trafficking and she will end up hurting thousands of people. You must complete this task before it's too late. Do you think you can become her friend before you kill her?" asked her mother.

"Of course I can, mother. I'm not an idiot. You trained me well. I will follow the plan as discussed. Tell me, how are you feeling?" Luna rolled her eyes at the question. Feelings weren't something she ever cared to discuss. Emotional or otherwise it didn't really matter to her. She was more irritated at her daughter for asking the question in the first place.

"The doctors tell me that there isn't much time left. Maybe six months, maybe not. But that doesn't matter. You get this job done before I die. Do you understand me?"

"Of course, mother." Mia felt the answer was adequate but also felt equally dismissed by her mother. She should have known better. But the question was more designed to find out a timeline to kill Cynthia more so than her mother's longevity.

Mia found Cynthia to be a lovely person, but Mia's hatred toward her kept her from truly becoming friends. Mia was from the 90's, as was Cynthia. Mia's chameleon attitude kicked in so she would fit right in with Cynthia's bubbly, airhead and caring demeanor. They went to several modeling gigs together as Mia learned all she could about her. Her parents were dead, no mention of siblings. She had no one but herself. This was perfect. As they were both extremely beautiful women, they decided to try modeling. They both got their own agent and began a modeling career. It took most girls years of experience to work as a model, but for these two, it seemed as if this was what they were destined to do. It was rather easy for both of them. On a cool spring afternoon they planned to have lunch together and share some great news.

"Hey you." Cynthia said with a grin as she sat down outside the café.

"Hey to you." Mia replied as she sat next to Cynthia at a table outside the front of the busy restaurant. The table was shaded by a large green and white umbrella. There were so many people walking by on the busy streets of Boston but no one paid them any attention. Both of them had wonderful news to share.

They ordered a drink and talked about the day's events, finally getting to the best part. They had both landed the opportunity for a million dollar contract with a big named firm modeling swimwear, lingerie, dresses and more. Each of them were happy for the other girl as they toasted to their new opportunity. Neither of them knew they were in competition for the same job just yet.

Two weeks before the final audition, Mia's mother passed away. Cynthia was very sad for her when Mia traveled back to Europe for the funeral. Mia's absence from the audition was not excusable, and Cynthia automatically got the contract. However, she rejected it. It simply wasn't right to take something that wasn't earned. Mia deserved a chance to say goodbye to her mother. Something Cynthia never got to do.

Mia arrived in Norway. Luna's white hair was a bit more gray, but still very beautiful. She hadn't died a bloody death as she always thought she would. Her career as an assassin didn't gain her any friends or trust with anyone. She was feared by those who knew her. She was a very lonely person. She wallowed in her own self-pity, never changing her outlook on life. It was always her choice to be lonely, growing older and eventually dying of cancer - a slow and painful death. She never married and Mia was her only daughter. Luna didn't really know how to love, including Mia. She simply looked after her and tried to teach her how to kill. After the first attack at Hugo's, Luna fled back to Mikhail's farm where she grew up. She knew she would be safe there. Mikhail always had a crush on her and they ended up sharing a bed together. She never told Mikhail about Mia. She didn't have the maternal instinct within her. Oddly enough, she ended up a lot like Hugo. Raising her own offspring without emotion or laughter. She was a lonely person. Her hatred toward Hugo never left. He had robbed her of a normal childhood, and she demanded her revenge by removing anyone and everyone from his bloodline. For many years she thought she had done just that.

One cool evening while walking through Oslo, she sat in a small, familiar café. Her glass of red wine was sitting in front of her as she read the local evening paper. She was older now, having aged very well and still able to turn men's heads. An older gentlemen walked up to her aided by a cane. "Excuse me. You remind me of a beautiful young lady I once met here. Her name was Mia."

"Inspector Solberg. How nice to see you again." She replied. The inspector smiled as he remembered their entire time together when they met. It was, to him, simply delicious. She was a vision of beauty in his memory. They had fabulous conversation, great wine and several wonderful evenings. They visited so many historical places and he was able to share more of his country's treasures than he ever had, and he had enjoyed every minute of it. She asked so many questions and he truly felt as if she genuinely wanted to learn. She was so refreshing. While his mind was reeling from seeing her again, Luna was pleasantly surprised to see him.

She also remembered her long, relaxing weekend with him. She knew she was looking for information, but since he offered it so soon, she knew she just had to spend more time with him so as to not give herself away. In doing so, the rest of the time they spent together was quite enjoyable. He made the weekend so effortless. He expected nothing from her but a new friendship. He gave her every bit of information she needed, as well as respected rapport without expectations. He took her to the most wonderful places and gave a historical journey that she never expected and would never forget. Despite her penchant for loneliness, she remembered this weekend as one her most favorite. She simply couldn't forget all the incredible information he gave her, especially since she was able to complete her mission.

At this unexpected meet, the Inspector was still full of information. Sitting at the lovely café, he continued to share some of the most historic information with her. Wild stories that even the most influential people of the country didn't know.

"Do you remember me telling you about President Truman coming to this country?"

"Yes, I believe I do." She replied. "He had something to do with the rebuilding process for much of the area here, did he not?"

"Ahhh. You have a wonderful gift of memory, my dear. You are correct. He was very gracious to infuse our country with finances so we could rebuild. And in the process, he was able to build the underground hospital below the airport. Sometime around the time that I met you, a rumor broke out that the hospital's security was breached. A young CIA agent was being shot at in several places throughout the town, and eventually ended up in the hospital with his pregnant wife."

"Inspector, do you expect me to believe all of your stories. Certainly an underground hospital run by the CIA would be a safe place." She said with a sly grin. She remembered every moment of that day.

"Of all the historical facts that I know, this is one I'm simply not sure of. But the story goes on to say that the agent's wife died that day. Of all the men around the world, his was the heart that was truly broken. They were very much in love. But all was not lost. The hospital doctors were able to save the child. It's a sad story to start but isn't that a lovely ending to...."

"What?" she interrupted. "The wife was dead and yet she had a child!" Her tone was that of anger and amazement.

The inspector was slightly shocked at her response but continued. "Well, my dear, it's just a story. The father was killed several years later and the child was eventually adopted. No one knows what became of her." Luna was still very upset, as even in death, Hugo still had a grandchild. No, it wasn't the child's fault, but Luna's revenge wasn't complete. The child would surely pay the price just for being in Hugo's family. They will all die – Mia will complete my mission - or so she thought.

The End

Be careful when you decide to start a project such as writing a book ~ especially when you're not really a 'writer'. This started out in a totally different direction! However, I hope you enjoyed it.

With a pencil and pad of paper in the back seat of our car in February 2013, the first words were written. Not long after, the pencil was replaced with a laptop.

I want to thank all the people along the way who were gracious enough to read the rough drafts over and over and over… And to my Uncle George for the art work…I truly appreciate it. I'm a work in progress. I'm new at this. But I started this project with intentions of writing a book about business practices and look what happened! Could it be that I should have written about those business practices instead? Maybe. Or probably! But writing a book and having it published it something on my own bucket list.

Write a book…Check!

Who knows what's next?

Do One Thing Every Day To Work Towards Your Bucket List!

55022330R00117

Made in the USA
Charleston, SC
19 April 2016